Book Early for Murder

Further Titles by Jennifer Jordan

A GOOD WEEKEND FOR MURDER
MURDER UNDER THE MISTLETOE

Book Early for Murder

Jennifer Jordan

BOOK EARLY FOR MURDER. Copyright © 1992 by
Jennifer Jordan. All rights reserved. Typeset by Hewer Text
Composition Services, Edinburgh, Scotland. Printed and
bound in Great Britain by Dotesios Limited, Trowbridge,
Wiltshire by arrangement with Severn House Publishers Ltd,
London, England. No part of this book may be used or
reproduced in any manner whatsoever without written
permission except in the case of brief quotations embodied
in critical articles or reviews. For information, address St.
Martin's Press, 175 Fifth Avenue, New York, N.Y. 10010.

Library of Congress Cataloging-in-Publication Data

Jordan, Jennifer
  Book early for murder/Jennifer Jordan
      .   cm.
  A Thomas Dunne Book"
  ISBN 0-312-06065-3
  I. Title.
PR6060.06247B6   1993
823'.914—dc20

With acknowledgements to
Joy Swift's Murder Weekend
Holidays

Chapter One

DEE

Holidays are important. Very important. Since the life of most married couples these days consists for most of the year of both of them going to work and back, preparing a meal and eating it, perhaps doing a spot more work, reading the paper, watching the telly, bath and so to bed, setting the alarm clock *en route*, there isn't much time for that companionship which, Agony Aunts assure us, is the foundation of a happy union. So when does this blissful togetherness get fitted in? Weekends and holidays, together with the gardening, shopping, household tasks, etc. and the relatives and friends that have to be seen sometimes unless one is to end up totally isolated.

I'm lucky. I've only got a part-time job, secretarial and general assisting in a letting agency. Which leaves plenty of time for keeping house, maintaining the body beautiful at Keep-Fit classes, keeping in touch with the odd (and the not-so odd) crony through phone conversations (always beloved of the female soul), lunch dates, after work drinks (with the office-bound) and brief visits to the home (of the house-bound). Then to greet the weary spouse with what one hopes is a sympathetic, comradely smile, a drink while the evening meal bubbles and simmers, and an adaptable readiness to either chat over whatever the post-working-day fancy pleases, or to fade tactfully from the scene.

But 'twas not ever thus. I can vividly remember the early days of our marriage, when I had predictably unpredictable hours as a frequently roving reporter with the magazine *Trends*. The local deli got to know us very well then, likewise the takeaway, and Barry did most of the home-prepared meals we had. And later, when I was a 'temp', and we'd moved into Elmtree Avenue in the good old London suburb of Woodfield, travelling home in packed trains after overtime at the oil company, or sudden crisis at the P.R. firm, to find that Barry had got tired of waiting and was setting out salad and baked potatoes *again*.

Well, we were poorer then, and needed all the cash we could get – also, I enjoyed the variety of my jobs. But it's nice now that the mortgage is paid off, Barry's job as a history lecturer at Woodfield Tech. is secure and a steady trickle of gold is coming into the coffers via payments, royalties and T.V. rights for Barry's spoofy crime novels. These started with *Proof of the Pudding* and *Penny for the Guy* and have continued with a faithful and growing circle of readers ever since. They've made Barry a minor celebrity – the kind of person whose name one has *heard* even if one isn't quite sure in what context – and they've provided us with luxuries like good wine, decent furnishings, holidays when we can get away, the occasional *objet d'art*, like the jade horse upreared on the table by the window in the living-room, and the not inexpensive maintenance of our much-loved little Schnauzer dog, Bella. So – I could afford to work part-time, or even give up entirely if I wanted to. And Barry and I are able to spend a bit more time with each other than your Mr and Mrs Average.

However, the onus is very much on poor Barry, who

now not only has a responsible and demanding full-time job, but an almost equally demanding part-time one, with deadlines. He's got long holidays, true, but apart from preparing new lectures, he also is expected to churn out yet another light-hearted mystery every year, which leaves holidays for 'research', relaxation, and sometimes starting the opus ahead of time. It's one of those impossible situations – Barry doesn't want to give up either his job at the Tech. or his writing – and I doubt if we could live on the writing alone, not in comfort anyway, even if I did a full-time job again. At the moment we're saving to buy another place somewhere and then let it out, so that in the future we could part-live on the proceeds and part-live on Barry's writing, with my contribution as the icing on the cake. Contingency plans, Barry says, are the hallmark of a shrewd politician. So we're being shrewd and politic.

Of course, as my ever-loving also points out, there's the possibility I might tire of the office scene and turn to insecure freelance journalism, or expand my so far insignificant efforts on the amateur dramatics scene into the full-scale production. Or go off the pill and have another go at starting a family. (Our last, in spite of frenziedly enthusiastic efforts on both sides, was unsuccessful, though apparently I'm a reasonably healthy specimen of womanhood and Barry's sperm count is perfectly normal). Whatever happens we're salting away against that li'l ol' rainy day, and meanwhile, as the most leisured and least-hassled member of the partnership, I do my best to do the 'little woman behind the great man' act, while retaining my own freedom and individuality. Namely, I do what I want most of the time, but make sure that Barry is warm, well-fed and comfortable, shielded as much as possible from the irritations of life and is provided with peace for his writing but chivvied by me about deadlines. I also act as reader, general critic and

3

supplier of occasional ideas, and ensure that we get abroad at least once a year and also get to see something of different parts of Britain. Our respective families are fitted into this schedule somewhere along the line, and we've still got quite a lot of friends who pop up here and there, from time to time. So, in its crazy way, our life-style seems to work.

Perhaps this long and rambling preamble will show you why holidays are important to us. And why, on a fine day in May, I was sitting cross-legged on the floor mulling over various brochures for July. Barry's term ends in mid-July and it seemed a good idea to get away as soon as possible for a break.

Bella trotted up, tail wagging, as I was comparing the delights of the Caribbean (brochure showing golden sands, blue skies and sea, and limbo dancers) and the Algarve (brochure showing golden sands, blue skies and sea, and horse-riding). 'Woof,' she said conversationally, nuzzled me and pounced on another brochure under the desk, which she brought over to me, carefully held between her little sharp white teeth.

'You're quite right, Bella,' I admitted, retrieving it. This one showed a panorama of Scottish lochs and highlands. 'I should be looking at the home scene first. It really is hard to choose, isn't it?' Bella gave me a sceptical, 'some people should be so lucky' glance.

'OK, you're right again. Let's go for a walk and think it over, shall we? Lake District versus Scotland; the Dales versus Cornish fishing villages.' Bella jumped up and pawed me. 'Now you're talking sense,' her approving bark told me.

We took a turn round the park, where Bella greeted sundry canine acquaintances and I greeted their owners and there was some fast and nifty footwork with a blue and red rubber ball, then ambled back along the suburban streets to Elmtree Avenue. It was definitely what I call Robert Browning time – 'Oh, to be in England,' etc., even though April was gone.

Our own front lawn boasted a border of daffodils and frilly narcissi, and a beautiful magnolia tree in the centre, now scattering creamy pink-hued petals over the grass. The rest was rose-bushes – which look great later, and last until winter, carefully planted. I could hear a ringing sound from inside as I inserted my key into the front door, and dashed into the hallway, nearly coming a cropper over Bella as I made a grab for the phone.

'Damn! Bella, move, will you? Hello?' But the phone had gone dead.

'Now look what you've done,' I told Bella severely. She looked impenitent and unimpressed. Bella knows that tomorrow is another day, and that anyone with urgent, exciting or titillating information to convey will have another go.

Sure enough, a quarter of an hour later, just as Bella had settled down with a bowl of Paws (she prefers Chunky Morsels, but the supermarket is out of them) and I'd settled down to milky coffee and an almond slice, the phone started trilling again. Bella gave me her 'See what I told you' look and I sighed.

'Just stop being so omniscient, you,' I told her firmly. 'Your name's Bella, not Wonderdog.'

'Hello? Hello? Is that Mrs Vaughan?' The voice, high-pitched and rather breathless, was not hard to identify. It belonged to Sharon, at Vista Travel ('Vista gives you the *big* view!'). Sharon was keen. Sharon was eager. Sharon had already supplied me with numerous brochures, showing happy holiday-hunting grounds from the Côte d'Azur to the Hebrides, from the Rockies to Reykjavik, from the heart of rural England to the middle of Mexico. Scenting the Vaughans as possible

5

long-term clients, Sharon was determined to please. She would leave no stone unturned to find us the new, the true, the well-tried and well-loved or the unusual and pioneering. Whatever turned you on, Sharon would get it – but the poor girl was having a hard time determining what exactly *did* turn the Vaughans on.

'Yes, Sharon.'

'Oh, you *knew* me.' She was pleased.

I forbore to point out that I didn't know anyone else with adenoid trouble, and merely said vaguely, 'The price of fame . . . '

'Listen, Mrs V.' Sharon was at her sales pitch again. 'I've got this cute little number that'll just *slay* you, I know it will. Well, it'll slay Mr V., anyway. It's something right up your street, with Mr V.'s novels and that. The only thing is, you've gotta book early or there isn't a chance, and believe me, you'll *kill* yourselves with disappointment if you don't get in. Your friend Mrs Zabrowki went to one and she thought it was just out of this world. "I haven't had such a good time in years, Sharon, is what she said."'

My interest was stirred. Zoe Zabrowski, uncrowned queen of Auditorium, Woodfield's leading amateur dramatic society, and wife of a food-chain tycoon. Zoe goes for the *outré* – well, she's been most places by this time. If Zoe liked it – well, that didn't mean that Barry and I would, necessarily, but it did mean that 'it' was probably piquant and worth consideration, at any rate.

'So give, Sharon,' I encouraged. 'What's this offer that's too good to refuse?'

'Well, you heard of Murder Trail Weekends, Mrs V?' Or not.' I frowned thoughtfully.

'You mean, where they book a hotel and hire a cast of actors to play a murder and the guests guess whodunnit?'

'That's the ticket. Only seeing as a weekend's not

very long, the company that does them has got together with another outfit and arranged a long, two-centre combo. You start at your first hotel, which is a nice Trusthouse Forte or Holiday Inn or whatever, and have your get-together and fun and games over the murder; then when everybody's in the spirit of the thing and enjoying themselves and nobody wants to go back home, you transfer to another hotel in the same area but in a more country setting, if you get me, with sports facilities and golf and ballroom and swimming pool and jacuzzi and . . . '

'Hey, stop,' I interrupted. 'It's OK, I get the picture.'

'Well, are you interested?' she demanded.

'We might be,' I offered cautiously. 'Don't worry, Sharon, whatever we choose, we'll book it through Vista. It's the least we can do after all your trouble.'

'Think nothing of it, Mrs V. It goes with the job.' But I could tell from her voice that she was pleased. 'And for your *abroad* trip . . . '

'Er – yes. Well, let's cross that bridge later, shall we?' I interposed hastily. 'Now, about this murder do. I think it *might* appeal to Barry, but of course I'll have to get the details first. It's highly expensive, I suppose?'

'So's mink, Mrs V.' Sharon came perkily back. 'So's oysters and champagne. So's a Rolls Royce. So's most of the best things in life.'

'Funny thing then that a guy wrote a song saying that the best things in life are free.'

'The best *simple* things, Mrs V. Them's freebies. Not the best non-simple things.'

'OK, you've made your point. I suppose you've got the relevant brochure?' Silly question. Sharon always has all available brochures, relevant or not.

'Right on.'

'Fine. Well, look, suppose I come in and get it, and

7

any more info. on tap, after I've had a bite of lunch. Say, two o'clock.'

'I'll be ready and waiting, Mrs V.'

'Oh, and Sharon . . . '

'Yes, Mrs V?'

'If you're ever wanting to sell the Eiffel Tower to someone, you can count on me for a recommendation.

I put the phone down and heard a plaintive 'Woof'. Bella was sitting at the foot of the stairs, looking forlorn.

'Oh, sorry, baby.' My heart and conscience smote me. Bella would have to go to the kennels, when we went abroad anyway. 'I forgot to ask about facilities for dogs. But I'm sure they'll fit you in. If they won't,' I said fiercely, 'we won't *go*, so there!'

'Woof,' returned Bella, mollified, and wagged her tail. She makes sure we get our priorities right.

BARRY

I drove slowly back towards Elmtree Avenue, along Oakdene Road, with the window down. At the top of a tree two birds necked and made low loving sounds to each other. Billing and cooing, it's called. I hoped they were turtle doves, but they may have been pigeons. Pink and white studded branches of apple trees undulated gently in the slight May breeze behind a tall wooden back-garden fence. An OAP with dapper blazer and fearsome eyebrows strode briskly along, brandishing his walking-stick. Round the corner of Larch Close, where bungalows and detacheds are found, a bulky man with floppy great hair and floppy white overalls was perched up a ladder doing something with a paintbrush to the casement on a mock-Tudor. He was whistling 'Greensleeves'. At the foot of the ladder white rock plants foamed against the riotous blues of forget-me-not and grape hyacinths. I remembered that the sincerest form of flattery is supposed to be imitation, which no doubt is why mock-Tudors are so popular. This was a nice one, and what with that and 'Greensleeves' and having taught the Tudors for a special paper this year, I began to think in terms of Stratford at half-term. Dee could do a couple of full days and a Wednesday morning at the agency and get away mid-week, coinciding with me finishing my marking and prep. And we'd have a glorious few days in the haunts of the Bard – wasn't there a garden there which had examples of every flower Shakespeare ever mentioned? I wondered vaguely what 'dewy eglantine' was like. I liked the sound of it anyway. Or was the eglantine Keats and not Shakespeare? He'd gone a bundle on nature, too. Dee would probably know – she's the Eng. Lit. one. In the meantime, we were lucky to be living at Woodfield, which so far had remained a relatively clean and graffiti-unbesmirched suburb with all the amenities one could wish for. And, it being the Bank Holiday weekend, I had picked up cooked chicken, sausage rolls and other goodies, with some Bordeaux, Mateus Rose and soft drinks, ready for a weekend spin in the Mini and a picnic.

'Yummy,' declared Dee, with a sign of contentment. I gave a slight belch, murmured 'Pardon' and let out my belt two holes. We lay back on the plaid car rug under a leafy tree in leafy Bucks, chewing blades of grass and watching the chequered pattern of sky and leaves overhead. A little stream wound and gurgled its way along, nearby, and Bella was cavorting in the field, chasing an imaginary rabbit.

'So how about Stratford?' I asked.

'Bliss. I'll find out what play's on. I hope it's *As You Like It* or *Love's Labour's Lost* or something. I mean, it's just not the weather for the tragedies. Though I daresay I could tolerate a good *Hamlet*.'

'Oh, Philistine!' I teased. 'By the way, Dee, I don't suppose you've got round yet to planning our July jaunt?'

'Some people are never satisfied! Barry, don't you ever think of anything but holidays?'

'Frequently,' I replied promptly, and proceeded to give a demonstration. Dee wriggled free eventually.

I didn't mean that – any anyway it's too soon after lunch, as that character in *Private Lives* says.'

She became businesslike, adjusted her hair, inspected a flawless complexion in a compact-mirror and delved into the recesses of her vast shoulder-bag, which is big enough to hold Miss Prism's three-volume novel of more than usual sentimentality, and then some. Finally she came up for air, brandishing a brochure.

'It's just the job, Barry,' she declared enthusiastically. 'Unusual, something we've never done before, and it might even give you an idea for the next novel.' I groaned loudly and at length.

'Spare me, oh hard taskmistress!'

'Well, if I don't chivvy you, Christopher will,' Dee pointed out with truth. Christopher Harcourt-Phipps is my editor, and he never lets up. To him 'writer's block' is a neurosis not to be encouraged.

'OK, OK, OK, I'll take a look.' There was a few moments' silence while I perused the blurb.

'Excelsior Two-Centre Holidays', it ran. 'Enjoy an exciting weekend pitting your wits and solve a puzzling murder! You may be baffled, bemused and bewildered, but you'll have to admit you haven't enjoyed yourself so much for ages. Every comfort is laid on – plus a team of first-class actors and actresses to play out this mind-tantalising crime! And after your efforts, relax in well-earned luxury in a glorious country setting, where you can play golf, squash, tennis, swim in the pool and enjoy the benefits of sauna and jacuzzi. Or just relax in the fabulous grounds and explore the country lanes. This is a holiday with a difference! But be warned – our holidays are extremely popular. So don't lose out – BOOK EARLY!' And more of the same.

'I suppose you have,' I said resignedly.

'Have what?'

'Booked early.'

'Of course not.' Dee was righteously indignant. 'I wouldn't do that without consulting you first!'

'But you're keen, aren't you?'

'Well – it does sound fun, Barry. Doesn't it?'

'Hmm . . . ' I murmured non-committally.

'They are terribly popular – everyone can't be wrong. And,' she concluded triumphantly, 'Zoe's been on one and *loved* it.'

'I suppose you got that straight from the horse's mouth'. (Not that Zoe's like a horse – she's more like a Maenad).

'Not exactly – Zoe's sunning herself at her villa in Turkey at the moment, so I couldn't ask her about it. But Sharon, at Vista Travel, swears that Zoe *raved* about it.'

'That's no recommendation,' I remarked nastily. 'Zoe would rave about anything that would keep her stage centre and in the limelight for five minutes.' I look somewhat askance on Zoe Zabrowski, who to my mind is one of the most tiresomely histrionic and self-dramatising females I've ever met. And you can strike out the 'one of'. However, Dee likes her, and I suppose we owe her a sort of debt of gratitude as she was instrumental in getting Dee's delightful niece, Sally, a place at the Edmund Kean School of Drama, where, by all accounts, she is doing extremely well.

'Oh, Barry!' Dee's face fell, and her huge green eyes turned cloudy. 'And I thought you'd like the idea. Never mind – I can soon find something else.'

I was a lost man. Sighing inwardly, I said, 'Don't bother, darling, I'm just making token noises. You're right – it's just the sort of off-beat thing we've never done and ought to do. I'm sure I'll enjoy it.'

'Really?' Dee peered at me suspiciously. 'You're not just saying that?'

'Truly I'm not.' And I spent the next few minutes playing devil's advocate and inventing reasons why I thought that damned holiday was the best thing since sliced bread.

'Just as long,' I finished up mock-ferociously, 'as we don't have to spend the rest of the summer holed up with Zoe in Southern Turkey.'

'Oh, darling, don't be silly,' Dee giggled. 'Much as I like Zoe and Stan, that *would* be a fate worse than death.'

'Talking of which,' I put in casually, 'just where were we when you started digging into that capacious handbag of yours?'

Some considerable time later, after considerable disarrangement of clothing, we summoned Bella from her antic activities and hauled the picnic hamper back to the car.

'Soon,' I stated, pronouncing the knell of doom, 'we're going to have to get a new car.'

'Oh, Barry! And he's been such a good and faithful servant. One of the family.'

12

'I know, Dee. But his innards aren't what they were, poor love. I'm afraid we've just about run him into the ground. One of these days we'll find ourselves stranded up the M-something at the mercy of a towing squad.'

Dee sighed gustily. She's strong on tradition.

'Not yet, though,' I promised, against my better judgement. 'We'll wait till the end of the summer. Unless we go touring.'

'If we buy a new car, we won't be able to afford to go touring.'

'True. Well, I guess he'll hold out till then.'

We got home without mishap.

I don't know quite why it is that I have misgivings about this projected July holiday, but misgivings I certainly have. It is partly something to do with large hotels, country houses, country clubs etc., but the other aspect is that we seem to have been drawn into amateur detection by force of circumstance. The first occasion this happened was at the never-to-be-forgotten birthday celebrations of Charles Wild, best-selling novelist, at Wentworth Hall, outside Woodfield, when our host was bumped off during a weekend we spent in company with his ex-wives, his mistress and sundry others who had no cause to love the great man. Even Chris Harcourt-Phipps, my editor, was briefly a suspect.* The second was at the Grange, an exclusive hotel in Sussex, where we spent last Christmas, and became involved in the Case of the Murdered Model, which was solved with our assistance.** The point I am making is that although I do very well out of my crime novels, I am nonplussed to find ourselves caught up in

* See 'A Good Weekend for Murder
**See 'Murder Under the Mistletoe

13

real-life detecting – and that seems to happen whenever we find ourselves at one of these plush places.

However, I am probably worrying unnecessarily. Why should our 'murder weekend', followed by a sybaritic relaxation, yield up a real crime? Looked at rationally, it is extremely unlikely. I shall give up these neurotic misgivings, and endeavour to enjoy myself at Dee's chosen holiday centre. After all, nothing drastic happened to Zoe, did it? So why should it happen to us?

Chapter Two

THE GATHERING OF GUESTS

'Looks like another fine day,' remarked Andrew Forbes, glancing out of the dining-room window of his Bayswater hotel. Outside a group of Indian ladies in saris fluttered and chattered, and several sturdy blonde backpacking Germans were making their purposeful way from the Youth Hostel to the *Bureau de Change* across the road. Outside the park, artists had put up canvases and a small straggle of passers-by had stopped to inspect them. One was bought by an Arab in flowing robes, who went off with it tucked under his arm. The bejeaned and hungry-looking seller had a satisfied smirk on his face, as well he might, for it had gone for four times its value, and he turned them out quickly.

'Yes – we're lucky for British July,' his wife Iris agreed. She poured out another coffee for them both, and smiled brilliantly at the good-looking young waiter who came to clear away the debris of their hearty British breakfast of bacon, fried eggs, tomatoes, sausages and mounds of toast. He blinked and gave a shy smile back. Andrew watched with amusement. He was used to the effect his wife had on people.

In her fifties, Iris Forbes was still a dazzler – with her smooth cap of white hair, heart-shaped face and beautiful complexion, and those amazing sapphire eyes. She gave an impression of both repose and outgoing warmth, and in truth, they were very well suited, with their natural zest for life. Andrew himself, with his leonine shock of grey hair, tanned skin and laughter lines, and burly figure just beginning to run to overweight, was what would normally be described as 'a fine figure of a man', and he wore the easy confidence of the successful man as casually as he wore his expensive Savile Row suits. They were Canadian – Andrew, from Scotland, had emigrated with his widowed mother as a boy and been educated by an elderly uncle in Toronto. With the demise of the uncle they had inherited his house and a certain amount of capital, but Andrew, eager to get up and go, had got himself apprenticed to a building firm at age seventeen and used his savings to buy a truck. Later, he had persuaded his mother to release some capital to buy four more trucks – and that was how his haulage firm had started.

The haulage business had boomed, and by his mid-forties Andrew Forbes was a multi-millionaire, director of various companies, with interests in property and hotels. He had a charming Scots-Canadian wife, Margaret, two fine sons, Malcolm and Duncan, a palatial British-style mansion in British Columbia, with the obligatory cabin by a lakeside for swimming and fishing, a shooting lodge in Scotland, and more money than he could spend in his lifetime. Then tragedy struck – Margaret had died, lingeringly, of leukaemia, and for a while this self-made and confident man had been like a boat without a rudder, desperately missing her calm commonsense and unfailing quiet support. That was where Iris had come in. Like himself, she had emigrated – in her case from the South-East of England – where she had trained as a nurse, and in Canada she worked for many years as a senior ward sister. Then she took up private nursing, and Andrew, laid up with a slipped disc and hating hospitals ever since his wife's illness, had been one of her clients. He had been, as she frequently assured him, a most difficult patient, and she had seen his worst and gruffest side. But, in the course of long days when she heroically kept him amused with chat, card games, and snippets of entertaining news, she had discovered his best, kindly, humorous side as well. When he was on his feet again and she had departed to another assignment, he was astonished how much he missed her, and with the singlemindedness that had characterised his entire career, he tracked her down and wooed her; with daily consignments of flowers, with delicious restaurant meals and evenings at the opera, which she loved, and theatre, which she loved only slightly less. His sons accepted her with enthusiasm, and Iris, who, unbelievably, had never married, found that a life with Andrew Forbes, strewn with luxury, made a very acceptable alternative to a career she was already weary of. She was alone in the world, her parents and sister having died, one by one, and she grew to love him. It was, everyone said, the perfect match – and for once 'everyone' seemed to be right.

Andrew, deciding he had worked hard and long enough, handed over his companies to his sons, still retaining a majority shareholder's interest; expanded his property deals, appointing managers to look after the nitty-gritty, and he and Iris now led a leisured life, spiced with constant travel. He realised, with some surprise, that he adored her, and, if possible, she was even more important in his life than Margaret had been. There was nothing, he told himself, he would not do for her. They were very happy.

In recent years they had not only travelled the length and breadth of Canada, and a good bit of America, from Washington to Mexico (where they both went down with gippy tummy) but had also toured Europe, either moving from hotel to hotel, or driving with their luxury caravan.

They had watched flamenco dancing in Spain (both eschewed bullfights out of principle), the Passion Play at Oberammergau, attended the music festival at Salzburg and sunbathed among the starlets at the Cannes Film Festival. They had listened to the Pope giving his blessing in St. Peter's Square and been rowed by straw-hatted gondoliers in Venice. They had ski-ed in Gstaadt and Val d'Isère, climbed to the Parthenon and taken the Orient Express to ancient Istanbul. They had bought gold bars in Geneva and been at Montreux for the Eurovision Song Contest. On the French side of Lac Leman they had stayed in the hotel where Byron had written 'Byron' in the register, and, asked for his first name, had grandiloquently added 'Lord'. They had supped beer in Bavaria and vodka in Moscow. They had ambled through Andorra and bopped in a disco in Budapest, ridden bicycles over the hump-backed bridges of Amsterdam and haggled over lace in Bruges. Eaten pastries in Demels in Vienna and seen the Can-Can at the Moulin Rouge. Trekked round the chateaux of the Loire Valley and luxuriated in the long, lovely summer in Provence.

But always, like homing pigeons, with the passion of the New World expatriate, they turned back to Britain. As Iris remarked wryly, tourists with money had the best of all possible worlds: service, comfort, good food. One could not quite ignore the evidence of overcrowding, industrialisation, dirt and graffiti, but one could wander off to the Tower or the Tate or the National Theatre, and not be seriously inconvenienced by it. They saw the sun rise at Stonehenge, were shaken by a towering Lear at Stratford, drove across Hardy country and relaxed in pretty Cornish fishing villages. In deference to Andrew,

18

Iris admired Scotland, but found Auld Reekie a trifle too grim for her taste, and the castle in Edinburgh, with its reminders of long, far-off forgotten things and battles long ago, a trifle disturbing, though she enjoyed the peace of the Highlands. Now it was a case of coming back to well-trodden paths. Which was why she was rather looking forward to their scheduled 'Murder Trail'. It would be new, and amusing.

'Let's face it, sweetheart,' she had commented, 'our palates are getting a bit jaded.' He had looked a little worried at that, and she hastily added, 'Not that I'm complaining! I adore our travels, and I adore being rich!'

'And no one deserves it better,' he had declared fiercely, his brow clearing. But she resolved to ring Malcolm in B.C. from the hotel that evening and enquire how the 'boys' and their families were getting on. Ever since the death of her sister (something which even now made her throat tighten with rage against a cruel fate) she had felt particularly alone and rootless, and not the least of the many blessings of her marriage to Andrew had been the ready-made family, complete with step-children. Not all the travel in the world could have compensated for loneliness, for the sense of 'not belonging'. Thank goodness, she had it all now.

'Let's go for a wander, when you've gone through the papers,' she suggested, and he agreed, smiling fondly at her.

Nora Hilton was also looking forward to her holiday week. Very much so. Holidays were treasured events in Nora's life. She was a widow, in what, in Jane Austen's time, would have been referred to as 'reduced circumstances'. Not that Nora was bitter, or envious – far from it. In fact, looking at the lives of her daughters and their generation, rushing from post to pillar and uneasily balancing jobs and families, she supposed she had been lucky. Twelve years of teaching had been followed by a safe, contented and uneventful marriage to Ernest, who was as old-fashioned as his name, and did not believe in married women working unless driven to it by dire poverty. Since Ernest earned a more than modest competence in insurance, Nora had spent the next sixteen years bringing up her daughters, Honor and Agnes, making the home comfortable and involving herself in such pursuits as the W.I., helping out at the Oxfam shop and corresponding with numerous scattered relatives and old school-friends. Ernest had caught a chill, developed pneumonia and passed away, leaving an unmortgaged house and three thousand a year in investments in the Abbey National. Nora had taken typing and shorthand at evening class, obtained a position with Ernest's firm, which did not have an age-barrier for typists, and seen her daughters through their final school exams, venture into the working world, and marriage. At fifty-four she had, in view of the increases in teachers' salaries, obtained another teaching job for three years, just to bring her infinitesimal pension up to one that was small rather than infinitesimal, and then, in a sudden excess of adventurousness, had applied for, and, much to her surprise, got, a job as a courier. She had always been good at French and German at school, and she was methodical, conscientious, efficient and pleasant, even in the most trying circumstances, like clients with hangovers and those who wandered off and got lost. Her daughters greeted her 'new lease of life' with mingled amusement and pride, and when, at age sixty, she had reluctantly decided the schedules were getting a bit much for her, she palled up with a lady she had met on one of the tours, who was running a home knitting business, and started turning out angora sweaters from home, with some home typing from an agency on the side – students' theses, authors' manuscripts, and so on. From time to time she let out a room at her pleasant semi in South Norwood, and, all things considered, did pretty well for herself. Time off, however, usually consisted of family visits and short stays with her old friend Doris in Bournemouth. Now in her seventies, she was deceptively sweet and fluffy-looking, with baby-blue eyes and a penchant for pastel colours – but with a soul that yearned for romance and adventure, even at second-hand. A casting director would have fallen upon her with sobs of joy if he had been looking for a Miss Marple – and in fact Agatha Christie was her favourite author – a fact that had weighed not inconsiderably when she had decided to forego her usual visit to Bournemouth and opt for the expensive but alluring Excelsior Holidays package instead. Her 'little grey cells', she considered, might not be up to the standard of Hercule Poirot's, but she was sure she had a sporting chance of solving whatever murder Excelsior might lay on.

Geoffrey Routledge sang 'Oh, what a beautiful morning, oh what a beautiful day,' slightly off-key, as he swung the tractor round in a final arc, swung himself off it, and trudged back to the old, capacious, inglenooked and tranquilly beautiful farmhouse he shared with his brother, Mark, and Goldie, the labrador. He was going to shower, shave, put on his slacks and Harris tweed jacket and sally forth for a pint or two and a game of darts in 'The Feathers'. Later, if he was lucky, that pretty little brunette he'd been chatting up last night might be in. He fancied he'd made some headway with her, and she did have the most delightful dimples, even if she was a bit Sloane Rangerish. Now what had her name been? Edwina, Davina – something like that.

Geoff was not only a Somerset gentleman farmer – he was everyone's idea of a gentleman farmer. Substantially built, with a fresh face and sun-streaked fair hair, he moved and spoke with slow deliberateness. In spite of a First in Agricultural Sciences and an impressive knowledge of the workings of the county (his family had been there for four generations), he still gave an impression of happy bucolic innocence. A gentle teddy-bear of a man, fully at home with calving and milk-yields and the production of root-crops and cider, he had a sometimes regrettable schoolboy sense of humour. A Hardy type with the patina of public school, Geoff was instinctively at one with nature. He fitted naturally into the rhythm of the seasons, and one felt that as the years went by, apart from a natural greying in the unruly hair, Geoff would remain exactly as he was. Men like Geoff Routledge were tilling the land in the time of the Saxons and when the Armada came, and, God willing, they would still be there in the twenty-first century, with their permanence, their certitudes, their distrust of foreign foods and foreign parts and their unshakeable convictions that if God wasn't an Englishman, then he jolly well lost out.

However, Geoff had his weak spots. One was an incurable susceptibility towards the female sex, especially manifested in an inexplicable attraction towards those members of it who were quite obviously unsuited to a life 'down on the farm'. His brother Mark joked about it, but privately worried, because Geoff was longing to settle down and start a family, but seemed immune to the rosy-cheeked buxom charms of Penny Bryant, who had set her cap at him ever since she was a toddler and he was a sturdy ten-year-old. Instead he sighed after blonde barmaids and cool, sophisticated London types; without much success, for they treated him indulgently and with a certain fondness, but without seriousness. If it had not been for his happy-go-lucky temperament, he might have got badly hurt. Another thing Mark found inexplicable and a bit eccentric was this haring off on some odd holiday where one spent one's time solving murders. As if there weren't enough problems in the world without fictional murders! And quite likely he'd find yet another unsuitable woman there and get hung-up on her. All things considered, it would be a great day for April Farm when Geoff got married at last – preferably to Penny Bryant.

'I'm very glad everything's turned out so well. Let's meet at Joe Allen's and have a drink on Friday, shall we – to a long and prosperous association', Karen Margolis purred down the telephone. Barely waiting for assent, she put the phone down, swung round in her black leather chair and fired out a series of rapid commands.

'Lucy, make sure the statistics on Olympic are up-to-date, will you? Ring *Time Out* and make sure that the Fishwives gig in Wapping gets coverage. Smooth the feathers of the Dental Hygiene Association and assure them they're uppermost in our minds. Get onto Ross Benson and lay it on thick about the aristos going wild about Eddie Orpheus and his Fifties look. And just check on what's happening with Mont Blanc, there's a love. You might ask Federico over for a drink and an off-the-record chat . . .'

'Yes, Karen,' sighed Lucy Dean, an Oxford graduate in Classics with slowish typing but impeccable presence, considerable ambition, a superb memory and a huge capacity for work.

'And Lorraine – when you've finished sorting through those press cuttings, just run round and give this note to Leon at Figure Fitness. Grab me a smoked salmon sandwich at Nibbles on the way back – oh, and get one for yourself and for Lucy, too. Plenty of lemon, remember. Book me a table for tomorrow evening at somewhere trendy but not too mind-bogglingly expensive – I leave it to your discretion. I've got *all* the guys from Balls Up to entertain. Send out this Press Release on Feminist Front. And if there's any time left after that, I've got some dictation I'd like you to take.'

'OK', grunted Lorraine laconically. She was a pertly attractive Cockney with six 'O' levels, superb speeds, a fiancé and a mortgage, and, like Lucy, considerable ambition and an infinite capacity for work (as long as it didn't go on beyond 5.30), though her memory wasn't too hot.

They made a good team. Karen had gone straight into secretarial work after school and an intensive commercial course, had firmly insisted on work in fashionable (though low-paid) Public Relations, and after honing her skills to impressive heights, had moved from a larger firm to become P.A. to Gillian Ames, a lady with many, many years in the business and many, many contacts. A well-heeled father had supplied her with the money to buy herself into a partnership, and later she had moved to start her own firm, Karen Margolis Public Relations. She took a couple of Gillian's best clients, Rushmore Business Machines, and Mont Blanc Ice Cream, with her. Gillian was resigned, even amused. Her husband had just retired and she was planning to get out herself in a year or two, anyway, and go and live in their villa on Ibiza. Karen had acquired several other clients of varying importance, and a small but fashionably-located office in the Covent Garden area, full of potted plants and cork-boards stuck with photos and memos and invitations. Her staff were lured by the draw of 'being in Public Relations' and kept by bonuses and free tickets, (which Karen frequently got given, for everything from fashion shows and gallery openings to previews of London shows). She was also liberal in the handing out of titles, such as 'Senior Assistant' and 'Personal Assistant', and generous Christmas and birthday presents.

At the moment, Karen Margolis Public Relations was doing extremely well, even in an overcrowded field. So much so that Karen even toyed with the idea of opening another office. Her most successful forays so far had been in the world of the rag trade, and she hoped for great things from these connections in the future. Of course, those who knew her well frequently expressed the opinion that Karen Margolis would have gone far, whatever she did. At school she had been Head Girl and a formidable member of the hockey team. She enjoyed marvellous health and had vast amounts of energy. She worked out three times a week after office hours at Figure Fitness; Perrier water was her favourite tipple, though she occasionally imbibed a Bloody Mary or a gin and orange, in the course of business. She made up for late nights by Sundays spent largely prone upon her bed with soothing eye-pads on, listening to soothing classical or light music. In appearance she was tall, Junoesque and ash-blonde, given to wearing smart suits with crisp white blouses, and chic black dresses for evening wear. With pearls. Her legs and ankles were superb and she rather resembled a television presenter. Although a go-getter already becoming quite a rich lady through hard work, drive, and shrewd investments, and with a streak of hard-core ruthlessness, she could be very kind, and had given, anonymously, large donations to starving children in Ethiopia and other causes. She believed wholeheartedly in the work ethic, in luck, and in the value of 'who you knew' as well as 'what you knew'.

Apart from family Christmases and of course her leisurely Sundays, the one time in the year that Karen Margolis firmly put work out of her mind was during her annual holiday. This year she had been invited for an

25

Aegean sailing holiday with her current beau, Graham, an investment banker and a keen sailor, but a tiff with Graham and something going wrong with the yacht put paid to that, and, in an uncharacteristically sulky mood, she had told Lucy to book her in for something unusual and fairly brief, since it was high-pressure time at the office and she intended to take the rest of her vacation later in the year and go winter-sporting. Lucy had come back with Excelsior's two-centre holiday, which intrigued Karen. The murder part of it would be amusing and a good talking point later, and the health and fitness fiend in her approved of the rest.

'Thank God!' Lucy had breathed to Lorraine. 'If she'd turned it down I don't know what I'd have done – there isn't *anything* else unusual except safaris in Kenya.' And they both unwound a bit at the prospect of a less hectic time than usual, with Karen off the scene.

Chapter Three

MORE GUESTS

Eric Coventry turned in at the entrance of the half-timbered Bell Hotel in Tewkesbury. Fronting the Avon and reconstructed in the late seventeenth century, this charming old hostelry was typical of what tourists looked for in English country towns. Eric, however, while fully appreciating his creature comforts, was immune to historic appeal. To him it was a convenient place for a jeweller with business to see to in Cheltenham – and convenient for receiving guests in the privacy of his room. If a couple of the guests seemed a bit Flash Harry for the setting, well, who worried about that these days.

Eric was a bona fide jeweller with a thriving business with three branches. He was intensely knowledgeable and sought, with great success, to give complete satisfaction to his customers. They got good value for money and expert advice. Eric and his staff would never try to persuade a young engaged couple to purchase a ring they could not really afford; and genteelly impoverished ladies seeking to sell cameos, or Victorian brooches and rings, always got a fair price. Moreover, Eric's appearance inspired confidence, as did his urbane but sympathetic manner. He looked like a noble Roman, with imposing profile and bald-pated domed head, fringed with dark hair. Stick on a crown of laurel leaves and he could have modelled for the head of a Caesar. But Eric had a sideline, and an extremely profitable one. Earlier days in London's Hatton Garden had served in helping him to build up a circle of 'contacts' – some of them, 'Fingers' Molloy, to name but one, of extremely dubious character. In short, though Eric did not go out 'on the job' himself, he had helped to organise some startling jewel robberies, and the disposal of the hauls thereafter. Now, as he packed his suitcase prior to departure, not only his jeweller's loupe was tucked away in a special hidden compartment, but also instruments for prising top-quality gemstones out of too-recognisable settings. The settings themselves, if they were gold, were removed by one of his accomplices – 'colleagues', as Eric called them – and deposited in a special place, rented under a false identity, to be melted down into nuggets of pure gold, which could be disposed of in the trade.

Eric was a loner by instinct – his wife had divorced him many years ago and remarried an uncultured but honest greengrocer. He did not miss her. Soon, after a few more hauls, Eric planned to retire from the business (and from his illegal activities) in comfort someplace nice and sunny. He already had a fairly palatial villa picked out (but he wasn't telling the locality, as he intended to make a complete 'clean break'), and several modestly substantial sums deposited in tax-haven accounts. Gloucestershire, even more popular since the advent of the Royals, with the county set, rich business people and whizz-kid weekenders, offered rich prizes, though sadly one's efforts had to be spaced out over a period time, for safety's sake. Eric was greedy, but not so greedy as to jeopardise his carefully-laid plans for an ill-judged rash of burglaries. Since his arrival, three weeks ago, there had been only one major country-house haul, at a manor near

Cirencester; though he had carefully earmarked two other places to be reconnoitred by his henchman. Eric was now off on holiday – a holiday which would bring him back to the area shortly, in a setting which would provide perfect cover and give him the opportunity to check on the reconnaissance. Dapper in his lightweight suit, he paid his bill at the desk, passed a couple of pleasant remarks with the clerk, and left tips which were more than adequate, but not large enough to arouse comment. It did not do to make oneself conspicuous, or act out of character. He had in a sense acted out of character three times before, with some discreet blackmailing – but the sums he had asked had not been large enough to impel his victims to go to the police, and he had asked for one lump sum only. One swoop was enough. To go back for more was foolishly reckless. On the whole, Eric thought he might enjoy this 'Murder Trail' idea, as well as its aftermath. Though a loner, he liked observing his fellow-men and women, not only as a hawk considering its swoop, but also as a detached observer. His favourite authors were diarists and essayists, his favourite dictum that of Bacon about 'hostages to fortune'. It was a mistake he had never made. There was no one he cared enough for to make a 'hostage' and when he disappeared, although he might at first slightly miss old associates, he had no doubt but that he would find ample compensations and some other outlet for his intellectual gifts.

'Well, I hope you enjoy your sleuthing, Dave,' joked John Potter, casting a quizzical glance at his flatmate, who was stretched out on the sofa watching a current events programme on television.

'Oh, I shall, I shall, don't you worry,' rejoined David Lydgate confidently. 'I'm determined to – and that's part of the secret of enjoying oneself, don't you think? I mean, if you embark on things with pessimism, you're not giving yourself half a chance. Whereas, if you're optimistic from the word go, something has to go badly wrong to foul things up.'

'Well, that's your philosophy, me old dear. For myself, I'm a dyed-in-the-wool pessimist. Fear the worst, that's my motto – then if you get the best, you're pleasantly surprised.' David smiled, but did not reply. He was dark-haired, tanned, twenty-eight, with fine-drawn good looks – one might have placed him as a business executive of some kind, rather than a civil engineer, which was his profession. He and the loud, rumbustious John had become firm friends while on a contract job in Abu Dhabi – a case of opposites attracting. They shared quarters in Abu Dhabi, a lovely villa some half-hour's drive away from their work, and had just completed the fourth year of their five-year contract. Both would be glad when the remaining year was up. Abu Dhabi was cosmopolitan, filled with Germans, Swedes, Canadians, as well as the British contingent, and it could be lively enough if you made friends easily, with lots of partying. Air conditioning in the offices and dwellings made the heat bearable, though in the nature of their work John and David spent a fair amount of time in the sweltering sun. The money was extremely good, too, though living costs were high, and both had managed to save deposits for homes in Britain on their return. Also, they were fortunate in that in spite of the dearth of work for civil engineering firms in Britain, their own was thriving, following an amalgamation, and they had jobs to go back to.

But after four years abroad, life there was becoming tedious. Some of the friends they had made had been coming to the end of their term of work shortly after they arrived – others had reached that stage by the third year there, and it was too much hassle to start all over again with new arrivals. Some, like Sven Larsen and Pete McKendrick, were moving on to other Gulf States; others returning to their own countries. And while there was no dearth of female companionship, particularly among the nurses, largely Irish, who were there mainly for mid-wifery, David had not got seriously involved with anyone. Unlike John, who played the field without, as he rather cynically observed, becoming involved in any paternity suits, David was a romantic. He knew that liaisons – and all too-frequently marriages, that were bitterly regretted later, on both sides – were frequently contracted through loneliness and being thrown together.

But David was looking for the girl of his dreams – although his dreams were rather imprecise on the subject, he had an unshakeable if perhaps naive conviction that he would know her when he met her. After all, all those lovely old songs, which his mother was so fond of, were based on that premise – and surely there was something in it. Now John, watching his abstracted look, guessed the tenor of his thoughts, and chortled.

'Who knows – you might find your ideal woman, as well as a solution to the mystery – never know your luck, do you?' David threw a cushion, rose, and advanced with mock ferocity, and John held a hand up in mock-terror.

'Pax, oh fierce one. I shouldn't tease, I know. I only do it to annoy.'

'Don't worry. I'm immune by now,' David retorted calmly. 'Your turn to make the tea, I think – or mix the drinks.' John consulted his watch.

'Sun's over the yardarm, I think. Right, what's your pleasure? Bourbon-on-the-rocks, or one of my specials?' David shuddered. John's last 'special' had laid him up for several hours with a throbbing head and Catherine wheels jumping before his eyes.

'Bourbon-on-the-rocks,' he said hastily.

31

'Your loss. Me, I'm going to mix a Chitty-Chitty-Bang-Bang for myself.' David shuddered again. He hated to imagine what the ingredients of a Chitty-Chitty-Bang Bang might be.

He usually spent his leave with his parents, retired in Jersey, but this time, apart from a duty visit, he and John had decided to join forces and rent a basement flat belonging to friends of John's, in South Ken. But first they were departing separately to do their thing. John to the South of France, where David suspected he was going to gamble away part of his surplus earnings in casinos as well as chatting up the demoiselles. John had an understanding with one of the Irish nurses in Abu Dhabi – Emer, a practical, cheerful girl with flaming red hair, freckles, a voluptuous figure and a numerous brood of brothers and sisters back in County Cork, not to mention an even more numerous brood of cousins in the States. She was, David thought, superlatively good wife-material for his friend, and John was thinking of naming the day fairly soon; but meanwhile he was relishing what was left of his bachelor status, and, with Emer safely stowed away on leave in the bosom of her family, as John remarked with a wink, 'while the cat's away the mice will play.'

For his part, David had decided on 'something typically English' and in search of this had been persuaded into the Excelsior Holidays two-centre holiday, which was certainly 'different'. Now he was not sure about its wisdom and even considered cancelling and joining John in Nice, but on principle stuck to his guns. Sipping his drink, he thought it would be ironic if John were right, and he met the right girl – though somehow he didn't see that happening. Probably the other guests would be middle-aged or elderly, though the young lady at the agency had assured him Excelsior were very 'with-it'.

*　　*　　*

Ellen Starr loved her flat. It was opposite the park at Queen's Park, which was bounded on three sides by Victorian villas, spruced up and charming in their way. The fourth side, Chevening Road, had big family houses. They were red-brick-faced on greystone, tall and untidily elegant, with sloping roofs and buttresses and long front gardens, which in Spring and early Summer swarmed with daffodils and other flowers, raggedy bright-green lawns, paving, sun-dials and odd stone ornaments. Through the windows evidences of individuality and taste could be glimpsed – tall bookcases filled with books, antique furniture, Japanese lanterns, pianos, a colourful rug hung up here and a child's kite there. Some were re-pointed and freshly painted, others genteelly shabby. They were the kind of houses people lived in in old-fashioned children's stories. In the park, there were usually dogs frolicking, their owners trailing behind, and squirrels leapt and chattered in the fringing trees at the borders. There was a children's playground, and it was quiet, apart from the cars whizzing by in the mornings, and uniformed kids trailing snail-like, unwillingly to school. This was an area which had been downmarket and was now upmarket – which was why Ellen's manager, Jason Purvis, had persuaded her to lease a flat on the top floor of one of the lovely old houses. It had been one of Jason's happier inspirations, and Ellen had moved in to the top floor of one of the very few houses converted into two flats. It had been filled with Victorian furniture – mahogany dining-table and chairs, wardrobes, a heavy large bookcase with glass doors, whatnots, even tables with bobble-fringed green cloths trailing to the floor, and an aspidistra (or its first cousin) in a brass urn. The owner of the house was a Victorian a nut. At first Ellen had not been at all sure this was the right ambience for her, but it grew on her, and now she loved its heavy, dark stillness. There were a few lighter touches of her own, mainly in the bedroom, and she had brought a few of her own ornaments from her parents' house – like the sad little porcelain clown, his cheeks streaked with tears, in 'On with the Motley' mood, and the exquisite statuette of a ballerina, a present from her great friend Meryl Sloan, now soaring to ever greater heights as a very young prima ballerina with the Royal Ballet.

There was a tranquility about the area she liked, though not far away a steady stream of traffic whizzed by into Central London, and the main-road shopping parade was undistinguished – though enlivened by touches like an old-fashioned Post Office and an old-fashioned shoe-menders. Ugly high-rises could be seen, on the way into the Edgware Road, and a constant surge of humanity poured into the station. But here all was quiet, cool. Which was necessary for her. Ellen Starr was a 'celebrity'. She was a pop singer who wrote most of her own lyrics; not a rock or punk pop singer, but something gentler, romantic with a touch of irony. She would have been good on the folk scene, but in an area filled with the American talents of Crystal Gayle, Tammy Wynette and the like, there wasn't really any opening for a British folk singer.

Ellen Starr was hard to categorise. You could compare her to the folk singers on the one hand, and people like Carly Simon and Lynsey De Paul and Kate Bush on the other. She had a pure voice, which could go from deep tones to high bell-like clarity and back again with no effort. In the music scene of the 1980s, she was uniquely herself, and her songs were both clever and poignant.

At heart, in spite of a veneer of sophisticated sangfroid, and the ability to protect herself in the abrasive world she belonged to, she was still a sweet old-fashioned girl, with dreams of the perfect lover, the ideal husband, and children. Plenty of time for that, Jason had insisted –

she was only twenty-four and a 'hot property'. She owed
a lot to Jason. He had made her – plucked her from
obscurity, accompanied her gigs, found her the best
musicians and backing group, dealt with groupies and
chased away unwanted, fortune-hunting hangers-on. He
had supervised her wardrobe, so that her beauty (long,
dark, hanging hair, slender but finely-curved figure, oval
Madonna face, huge fringed brown eyes) was shown to
best advantage; simple white blouses and jeans, clinging
silk jersey in black and subtle colours, gorgeous peacock
and scarlet prints, drifting virginal white. He had found
her this flat; protected her privacy. A couple of times
he had mentioned marriage, and she had thought 'why
not?' He would continue to manage her – after all,
there were plenty of examples of husbands making a
career of managing their wives. Look at Elkie Brooks,
Dolly Parton, Cilla Black, to mention but a few. But
something in her balked. Jason had his own dream.
He was the 1960s man in a 1980s world; determined
to recreate the conditions of the 1960s successfully; the
meteoric entrepreneur, making his mark and hopeful to
become a millionaire in the process. Though he was
fond of her, and she of him, it was Ellen Starr the
singer, the personality, he sought; not Ellen Starr the
woman. And he managed other artists as well – any
one of the up-and-coming young women, she knew,
would suit his purposes as well as her. Moreover, Jason
was a hard taskmaster, and she did not see him in
the father role. Children, to Jason, were accidents of
nature – he would not accept the need she had to stay
at home with her own children, be a proper mother.
No – any children she and Jason might have would
be consigned to nannies and boarding schools, while
Ellen Starr continued her public appearances, her love
affair with live and television audiences. This was not

what Ellen wanted. Somewhere, sometime, she felt, her prince would come, and with a certain practicality she was already building up her career as a songwriter – something which she could continue without too much difficulty if she had a husband with whom she had to, say, travel at times, or who wanted her home to prepare dinner instead of being on the road to Liverpool or Berkhamstead or Glasgow.

One thing she was grateful to Jason for was that he recognised her need for holidays, and never interfered with it. Last year she had been in Spain, sunning herself blissfully; this summer she was going on this weird Excelsior do – somewhere, she thought, with an imp of mischief, where the other guests might not even have heard of Ellen Starr, and she could be Miss Anonymous, blissfully unknown and just out to have a good time. How much of a good time remained to be seen. It was unlikely, she reflected regretfully, that any tall dark handsome stranger would be there. More likely OAPs. Oh well. She would take her new evening dress anyway – the one with the rainbow panels. And her old-gold embroidery-encrusted caftan. And the emerald velour pants suit. Shorts for tennis, track-suit for jogging and work-outs. And the peach nightgown and peignoir *and* the decadent black silk pyjamas, for nightwear. Oh yes – and the violet chiffon.

She visualised a courtly old gentleman bowing over her hand and saying, 'May I have this dance, Miss Starr?' and giggled.

'Looking forward to the holiday, love?' Ron Fairclough asked his wife, Linda. They were sitting out in the garden enjoying a drink while in the kitchen the Sunday roast spluttered and sizzled in the oven. The garden was a pleasant sight. Manicured green lawn (Linda's work; she was energetic), crazy-paving path and oval flowerbeds round the side, with a couple of spreading trees to give shelter and added privacy at the bottom.

'What do you think?'

'I'd think yes.'

'And you'd be right.'

'Sorry it's not abroad this time, but there've been a lot of expenses lately. Never mind – South of France next year, hey? I've always fancied a look at the Riviera.'

And, after a lot of hard work, he could afford it. From the North, Ron had transplanted to London – work for plumbers was plentiful. He took a pride in his work, and had been heard to say frequently that one of the marks of a highly-developed country was its excellent plumbing – a view which many people, who had endured the loos in certain Continental countries with resignation mixed with horror, agreed with. In due course Ron had become a partner in his firm, and after more steady work – a great deal of it – he had been able to buy the roomy detached house in Loughton. A good place to be, he thought with satisfaction; near to the City by car or train, a decent shopping parade with pleasant pubs, and green fields on the outskirts, giving that country feeling. It was a far cry from the two-up, two-down in Doncaster where he'd spent his boyhood. Now, with all the eagerness of the newly-affluent, he was anxious to enjoy the fruits of his labours, and give Linda a good time. A thickset man with greying fair hair, he looked stolid, dependable, and very English, which he was. Linda was a Londoner, born and bred, from Deptford. He'd met her at a party where she'd laughed, not unkindly, at his clumsy efforts at disco-dancing, but seemed interested in talking to him. She was – as he found later – interested in everything and everybody. She was a Cockney sparrow, shrewd, realistic, but kindhearted and with a good sense of fun. Like himself, she knew how to enjoy herself wholeheartedly, and she had a restless energy that sometimes left him exhausted, thinking nothing of being up till all hours and then in to work spruce and on time and on the ball next morning. She'd worked as a typist and occasional book-keeper in a firm that manufactured shoes. Not the most exciting job in the world, but it suited her. He'd been worried by the difference in their ages – he was now forty and she twenty-three – to make sense of previous – but she just laughed and told him not to be stupid; there was plenty of life in the old man yet, and she knew a good thing when she saw it. Eventually, with much prodding from Linda, he had proposed, and had never since ceased to be amazed and delighted that she had accepted him. Thin, with long marvellous legs, blonde hair and a pretty face, complete with tip-tilted nose, her appearance and her gay spontaneous laughter turned heads; and she was a worker, too, insisting on helping with the books and acting as occasional receptionist at the office, filing bills and keeping careful records, as well as running this house, without help, and doing the garden. And laughing off the whole as a labour of love, pointing out that she couldn't stand to be unoccupied and the role of 'just a housewife' didn't suit her. It was she who had chosen this holiday, which she saw as a delightful novelty.

She had been only half-joking when she said she knew when she was on to a good thing, for life with Ron represented the nearest thing to luxury that Linda could imagine; but she loved him genuinely, though being 'in love' was to her something that existed purely in Mills and Boon novels (of which she read a large number).

Life was for living, and one just got on with it without undue fuss – the same applied to marriage. One took the rough with the smooth, and stood by one's man,

38

if he was a good one, which her Ron was, thank goodness.

And, of course, if there were good times, one enjoyed them for all one was worth, just as one had endured the hard knocks. As for money, if one didn't have much, one didn't make a song and dance about it. If one did, one enjoyed it, and gave some to family. After all, that was what money was for, wasn't it? Making people happy. If it didn't, she didn't see the use of it. It made *her* happy, and that, she considered, was because she had a proper outlook on life. Just now she thought with pleasant anticipation of the holiday they were going on. She hoped they'd meet some nice people, and she hoped that Ron would enjoy it as much as she intended to.

'Take five,' the organiser of 'Murder Trail Weekend, July' intoned wearily. 'And then, once more with feeling.' He didn't look or sound as if he could do anything with feeling himself, Stephen Marriner thought. He looked washed-out and hung-over, and his voice had a hopeless graveyard timbre.

That might have been in part due to Madeleine Lang.

'She shouldn't have been called Madeleine, she should have been called "Maddening",' one of the cast had opined, and it had not been a weak witticism, but a heartfelt statement of true feeling.

They were rehearsing in the hotel for the forthcoming 'Murder Weekend'. Maddy Lang was the *enfant terrible* of the cast. Opinionated, bumptious and a tease, she had managed to get up everyone's nose, tossing her dark hair about and making malicious remarks. The only daughter of rich parents, she had got through drama school, done some amateur work and had parts in farces – one of them had been a Ray Cooney which had subsequently had a successful run, which Maddy never tired of informing

39

them – she had quitted the cast after a year to 'get experience' so as 'not to get stale'. Maddy might not be exactly a veteran, Stephen thought ironically, but at least she was well fitted for two parts – the *ingénue* and the bitch. The former by training and the latter by natural inclination. He momentarily toyed with the image of Maddy as Goneril – or Regan. He was willing to bet she'd be superlative in either role.

And he should know. For a while Stephen Marriner, undeterred by the dire predictions of family and friends about the high incidence of starvation in the acting profession, had taken Shakespearian parts – graduating from First Messenger and Attendant Lord to Lysander in *A Midsummer Night's Dream* at Regents Park, then Bassanio in *The Merchant of Venice*. His biggest breaks had come with a fiery Hotspur in *Henry IV* and Orlando in *As You Like It* with the RSC, and he had played Kent in *Lear* and Horatio in *Hamlet* at Stratford.

Then there had been a fallow, and horribly long, period, when Stephen had ruefully discovered the truth of what his family and friends had said, and had found it inordinately hard to pay the rent of his modest bedsitter and keep body and soul together. He had joined the dole queue, and he had done various other things he wasn't proud of, including accepting frequent sums deposited in his bank account by his sympathetic mother; learning that the rules of survival for an actor are a) to keep eating – not much but enough to sustain life, and b) to get work, *any* work: including a spell as a male stripper under the pseudonym of 'Paolo, the Italian Stallion' (with mental apologies to all Italians). Perseverance had paid off, and he had found supporting roles in the provinces, Sir Fopling Flutter (very camp) in a Restoration piece, and, finally, television, where he had played a harassed husband in a totally forgettable situation comedy (the situations were

incredible and the comedy was of the hopeful kind);
the Earl of Essex in a play about Good Queen Bess,
a psychopath in a mystery play, and a swashbuckling
character called Adam Derwent in a mystery series set
in Corfu. The latter had brought him to the attention of
various people, and purely, he felt, on the strength of
his carefully-manufactured quizzical smile he had, in the
face of considerable competition, landed the plum role of
'The Baron' in a remake of the television series about the
John Creasey character.

Now, having sold his soul to 'The Baron' and waiting for
the next series to come up, Stephen was a veteran of the
theatrical profession, and more than somewhat cynical.

In appearance, he was just above average height,
undeniably handsome, with a mobile face and expressive
eyes, reddish brown hair and a fashionably lean torso,
which he kept in condition with workouts. He also had
a sense of humour, wit and a good education, with a bias
towards the arts in general, and an excellent memory.
The 'The Murder Trail Weekend' had cropped up in a
'resting' period; and since the concept intrigued him and
he had worked for them before, he was prepared to give
it whatever he could.

With the exception of Maddy, he quite liked the cast.

Tea and biscuits had been brought in for sustenance,
and he helped himself to a steaming cup, and a plateful
of Rich Tea, dispensed by Melissa Stirling, Excelsior
Holidays rep; known as 'Lissa' to the cast, and one of
the good things about this jaunt. Maddy wandered over
and crunched a biscuit with an expression of devilment
on her face.

'Is that a gun?' she asked in carrying tones, staring at
his crotch. 'Or are you just please to see me – as Mae
West once said.'

'It's a gun all right,' Stephen replied, from between

clenched teeth, 'and, no, I'm not pleased to see you, Maddy. Is anyone?' Undeterred, she trilled an amused laugh, and wandered off.

Stephen exchanged speaking glances with Melissa, who smiled sympathetically.

'I should think you'll be ready for your break,' she said, 'relaxing in idleness. If only to get away from *her.*' Stephen smiled back.

'You bet,' he replied in heartfelt tones. 'I'm looking forward to it already.' He looked with approval at Lissa, radiating efficiency from her gleaming chestnut pageboy to her polished patent-leather high-heels, and felt glad that she would be there, on the second stage, as well as a load of people he didn't know. He wasn't quite sure, as yet, that joining up with the guests was going to be a good idea.

Maddy was not, as they thought, out of earshot. She shot a jealous glance at Lissa; 'Miss Sweetness and Light', she had christened her. A speculative expression took over her pretty face. She was really quite attracted to Stephen Marriner, and regretted that she had got off to a wrong start with him. It would, surely, be a comparatively simple matter to book for the second part of the two-centre holiday. Unless all the places were taken. After all, Stephen had done it, obviously. Perhaps she could get onto a better footing with him – show him her nicer side. She *had* a nicer side – not many people realised that it was nervousness and basic insecurity that made her show off and act as she did. If there were any difficulties, a bit of string-pulling could fix it, as it had done for Maddy all her life. She was just lucky that she had talent enough to justify the string-pulling. Pity Lissa was going to be there too, but it was her job, and even Maddy had to admit she did it well.

'Oh well,' Maddy thought, 'this holiday might throw up a few surprises for you, Stephen Marriner.'

42

Chapter Four

'MURDER TRAIL' WEEKEND DEE

As it happened, the poor old Mini gave up the ghost before our holiday. More with a series of whimpers than a bang, finally sliding to total immobility outside Sainsburys. It had to be towed away to our local garage, where they pronounced it a write-off, but offered a token sum, as they could dispose of some of the parts. I gave it a parting, sympathetic pat on the bonnet, and walked away, feeling quite distressed. That Mini had been part of our lives for a long time now.

Barry, however, was quite bucked up at the prospect of choosing a new limo – this took hours of consultations and try-outs, which I found boring, but which Barry revelled in. Eventually, having secured my agreement, he settled on a silver-grey Volvo which was roomy (with a special bucket seat for Bella in the back), hardwearing and smooth-running. It also, as I wryly pointed out, was eminently suited to our age-group and image as 'Young Urban Professionals'. (Well, I'm not exactly a professional, but Barry is, even if history lecturers don't fit into the Yuppie framework as cosily as bods who do something undetermined and unspecified

43

in the City). Barry retorted that in a few years we'd be Muppies (Middle-Aged Urban Professionals) if not Mop-Outs (Middle-Aged Drop-Outs) so we ought to make the most of any courtesy title which had the word 'young' in it. I must admit both Bella and I enjoyed our runs in the Volvo, which glided along swiftly and effortlessly and without the starts and stops, snorts and belches which the late-lamented Mini had been prone to. Maybe by the time Barry and I are Mop-Outs we'll be rich – one would, after all, prefer to Mop-Out in comfort than in penury. Barry seems gloomily certain he'll be axed within the next few years in the education cuts sweeping his borough, and I can't see him having the heart to start from scratch all over again away from Woodfield Tech., so it looks as if prosperity is going to depend on his writing in the future, plus whatever money-making talents I can muster. And although my dear better half loyally assures me on numerous occasions that my talents are multifarious, they do not seem to be of the money-spinning variety so far.

The day we set off on the first stage of our two-stage holiday, (the 'Murder Trail' part), was medium bright, but with the odd shower threatened by the BBC weathermen. The hotel, called simply The Hall, was in Hereford & Worcester, vaguely between Ledbury and Malvern. It was set amid lush green fields and had a great long driveway which skirted a newly-erected Children's Fun Playground, complete with water-chutes and a big wheel and a mini-railway and all manner of stalls and games. The Hall itself was large and ultra-modern, with marble pillars, chromium, split-level coffee lounges and a large cafeteria. There were two large car parks and a nightclub and even a few small shops around a central courtyard.

We parked the Volvo in one of the car parks and checked in. We were assigned a room on the second floor. The snooty hotel receptionist raised an eyebrow at Bella, but she was patted enthusiastically by the Excelsior Holidays rep., an attractive girl in a black suit and white blouse, with gleaming chestnut hair in a pageboy. She held a clipboard, which she duly ticked, introduced herself as Melissa Stirling, usually called Lissa, and explained that after we had settled into our room we would be required to attend a pre-dinner gathering in the foyer of the 'Banqueting Room', which was in an annexe off the courtyard where the shops were. And would we remember to wear our 'something brown' (which we'd been informed about in previous 'Murder Trail' literature) which marked us out as members of the 'Murder Trail Weekend' group? We replied that we would. In fact, we'd already received a timetable of the week's events and a brief outline of the situation which supposedly had brought all the guests together.

I will not go into this; suffice to say it was extremely complicated, and as time passed, with ingenious games, a disco, a treasure hunt and other activities, somehow the 'story' unfolded and we met the members of the cast in their allotted roles.

There were about a hundred guests – more than we'd anticipated – some *habitués* of 'Murder Trail' weekends, but most, like ourselves, new to the game. A board was put up before dinner with the names and places for each table. Tables were large and long, and, by some inspired quirk of organisation, we were seated with the other people who had booked for the two-centre holiday and therefore would be coming on afterwards, like us, to the second hotel.

In the course of dinner and the ensuing games and dancing, we exchanged names and some information about ourselves. Barry and I quickly spotted the young pop singer, Ellen Starr.

'Now, come on, Ellen, don't try to keep on kidding us you're a secretary. We do watch television, you know!' Barry pointed out. Ellen shrugged and gave an 'Oh, well, it was a good try' sort of smile.

'I give up,' she said. Her speaking voice was beautiful as well as her singing voice. In fact, she was rather beautiful all round. The men in the party certainly seemed to think so, particularly a fair-haired young West-countryman called Geoffrey Routledge.

We soon found Barry had an ardent fan, in the person of Nora Hilton, a sweet little old lady in the Miss Marple mould – not only in looks, but also in the penetrating comments she made on Barry's plots.

'I'm a crime novel buff – like a lot of other people, I suppose. And of course there are so many good authors that it's impossible to read them all. Even though I've plenty of time and my local library is really remarkably good. Are you writing another, Mr Vaughan? Oh dear, I suppose that's the one question guaranteed to irritate.' She looked so sweetly penitent that I rushed in.

'Yes, Barry – what about the next book? Somehow I don't seem to have heard much about it recently.'

'Er – well. It's in abeyance. I'm waiting for inspiration to strike.' Ellen Starr nodded understandingly.

'I know the problem. It's the same thing with my songwriting. Some days it's there, some days it just isn't.'

'Well, darling,' I said briskly, 'I expect inspiration will strike sooner or later. Preferably sooner. Like after our holiday.'

'I bet Agatha Christie wasn't chivvied like this.' That got a general laugh.

'Agatha Christie made use of her holidays. I mean, she didn't just go on archaeological digs with Professor

Mallowan, she produced gems like *Death on the Nile* and *Murder on the Orient Express.*' Barry gave his long-suffering sigh. It's an old acquaintance of mine.

'Women! You see how she nags me?'

'Join the club! Still – we love 'em, don't we?' It was Ron Fairclough, the plumber. He seemed pleasant but rather heavy weather. One of the lads. Most of the party had seen the TV series of Barry's stories, called *Whodunnit* and there was discussion of that and of the actors involved. I took rather a dislike to a Mr Eric Coventry, who made a few what I thought of as barbed double-edged remarks, but Barry didn't notice – or pretended not to. He's more naturally polite than I.

After that, conversation turned to items in the news, and after coffee we drifted off to dance. I was being partnered by Andrew Forbes, a rather dishy but high-powered Canadian, and Barry was dancing with Karen Margolis, a public-relations executive, also high-powered, when one of the other hundred-odd guests rushed in and called, 'Someone's been killed out in the lobby!'

'Ah,' Andrew murmured with a smile, 'Action at last!' We rushed out to find one of the cast lying on the floor with a stage dagger stuck in her chest and some very red, very messy stage blood in a very large patch around. Those at the bar explained excitedly that she had come staggering in from the courtyard with the dagger stuck in her, and collapsed on the floor. Now was our time to start interrogating the cast about alibis and motives, as 'police' circulated, taking statements, and the 'body' was borne off in a real ambulance. Our 'Murder Trail Weekend' had begun in earnest!

The next day we discovered an 'incident room' with a noticeboard and table containing many and varied clues. Cast members were wandering round being inter-rogated by guests, and it was getting more complicated every minute. I got tired of trying to quiz people, collected Bella and slipped off into the Children's Fun Playground. I was just coming off the Big Wheel, when I saw a familiar person, a blissful smile on his face, chugging round the mini-railway. The smile faded as he noticed me.

'Having a good time, Barry?' I enquired.

'Er – yes. See you on the water-chute in ten minutes,' he shouted, as the carriage he'd squeezed himself into vanished into a tunnel.

We got rather wet riding boats down the water-chute. So did Bella, whom I'd brought along for the rides, but it didn't stop her yaps reaching hysterical ecstasy.

'Bella, cut it out,' I commanded. 'Enough is enough.'

She shook herself vigorously, liberally sprinkling my dress with water-drops, gave a naughty bark, and scampered off towards one of the 'policemen' who was striding towards the nearer of the two car parks. Like Bella, various 'Murder Trail' guests were scampering in his wake. Barry looked at his watch.

'We're five minutes late for meeting in the incident room to start the treasure hunt. Methinks another murder has taken place.'

'Methinks thou mightest be right.'

The second corpse proved to be that of a boorish character called 'Edward', uncomfortably squashed into the boot of his car in the car park. Again, stabbed. After the 'corpse' had been driven off by a 'police officer', accompanied by the 'weeping wife', there was tremendous chatter, grouping and regrouping among guests. I noticed Nora Hilton and the Forbes couple conferring. I'll say this for the 'Murder Trail Weekend' – everyone was very friendly. Proving that there's nothing like a good old phony murder to break the ice. Real ones tend to have a different effect, of course.

When it was announced that the treasure trail would proceed as planned, but was not compulsory, Barry looked at me and I looked at Barry and we both looked down at Bella, who wagged her tail in agreement. As a family, we were as one. 'I vote,' suggested Barry, 'that we cut out and go for a spin in the car and have lunch out.'

'But what if someone else gets "murdered" while we're away?'

'Never fear – Sherlock is 'ere. I'll get Nora Hilton to tell all on our return.'

'I'm not sure that's quite ethical.'

'Stuff ethics. Anyway, my guess is that the next murder will be this evening. It's not artistic to have them too close together.'

'You've got a point there. OK, take Bella – I'll meet you at the car. Just popping up to our room to freshen up and get a cardi.'

As I got out of the lift I caught sight of 'Edward', now clad in jeans and a sweat shirt proclaiming, 'The N.T. is the Tops', fitting his key into the door of the room two along from ours. I galloped up before he'd a chance to disappear inside.

'Hey! You're meant to be dead!' He turned with a rueful grin.

'Foiled! Please don't tell anyone. Of course, once we're killed off, we have to lie low till Sunday morning, when the solution is given and all the cast reappear. But I'm afraid I cheat and nip out for a breath of air if the coast is clear. Actually, I just came out to borrow some cigarettes from the other 'corpse'. She's installed on the first floor. I've only been installed for ten minutes myself!' All trace of the boorish act he'd put on as 'Edward' had disappeared.

'You weren't very nice to me when I tried to ask you questions,' I said reproachfully.

'Sorry. That wasn't me – that was Edward, you know.

We have to act our parts. In fact, we really get to believe in them while we're doing them. If you like, I'll tell you more about the whole set-up on Sunday morning. After the revealing of the solution, we chat to the guests in our own characters – if they want to chat to us, that is. I'm afraid I can't tell you anything about the solution, except that it's very complicated. I'm Stephen Marriner, by the way.'

'And I'm Dee Vaughan. Where do you get your plots from?'

'Make them up ourselves. Have loads of meetings and pool ideas. Scour round frantically for things we can use as clues.'

'Like the newspaper articles and the "mug shot" of Edward.'

'That's right. It's fun, but very hard work. Different, though. We all love it. Well, I mustn't delay you . . . '
I took the hint.

'See you on Sunday morning then. Er . . . do you need anything, while you're pent in durance vile? Seeing that we're just along the corridor.' His face brightened.

'Angel of mercy! If you could see your way to slipping me in another packet of ciggies and some plain salted potato crisps, I'd be eternally grateful.' He fished a couple of pound coins out of the pockets of his jeans, and I took them.

'Right you are. I'll knock twice and whistle the Harry Lime theme, so you know it's me.'

Amused by the exchange, I collected my cardigan, put on lipstick. Barry was looking aggrievedly at his watch as I slid into the car.

'Sorry I took so long! I was just having an encounter with a corpse.'

'Well, next time make it a briefer encounter, will you?'

50

'I'll try to. Don't you want to know whose corpse?'

'There are only two to choose from,' Barry pointed out. 'The awful Edward?'

'Spot on. His real name's Stephen Marriner, and he's rather nice, out of his Edward character, that is.'

'Nice enough to give you the solution?' I was shocked.

'Barry!' I protested indignantly. 'Would I ask a thing like that?'

'No,' Barry admitted.

'Humph! Some of us have a conscience, you know!'

'Well, anyway, I reckon I've got it partly worked out,' the infuriating man announced smugly. 'And I bet you anything the next corpse is . . . '

'Oh, shut up!'

*   *   *

We lunched in Malvern, home of Malvern spa water and the Malvern Festival, which had been going on a few months back. Above the sloping streets of the small town, huge tussocky outcrops of land loomed towards the sky. Nice for walks, if you happened to be a goat or a mountaineer. The hotel was an old coaching inn, with picturesque lacy iron balconies decorating its white frontage, and had a balcony set out in chess squares with giant chess pieces, overlooking a pretty sloping garden. Afterwards we walked downhill to Priory Park, and shared some After Eight mints sitting by the small ornamental lake.

There was an Alan Ayckbourn comedy on in the little theatre, and we looked in at the foyer, paying our respects to the portrait of George Bernard Shaw, who had declared Malvern to be 'this most English of towns' – or words to that effect. By which time it was definitely time to be

51

getting back to the happenings at The Hall. We ambled in a downward direction again (everything in Malvern seeming to be on a near vertical slope) towards the car park near the station, where we'd left the Volvo. Huge Victorian mansions stood sedately side by side along the road, and my brain, which has developed a cash-register facility where property is concerned, ever since working at the letting agency, began to ring up the hundreds of thousands. Suddenly something stopped my in my tracks. Barry, who was in my wake, cannoned into me.

'Dee!' he exclaimed reproachfully. 'Must you make these unscheduled stops?' In answer, I grabbed his arm, and put a finger on my lips.

'I see someone,' I hissed. 'Look!' Barry obediently looked. Round the corner of one of the big houses came the man who had been sitting at our table the night before – Eric Coventry. He looked very dapper and smart, but was accompanied by a shabbier, thinner individual with lank hair growing over his collar and the look of a downmarket ferret. They stood surveying the side of the house which, as well as a large window with stained glass panes half-way up, boasted an ugly circular fire-escape on the exterior.

'Hmm,' Barry murmured in my ear. 'Obviously we're not the only ones who don't appreciate treasure hunts.'

'Shifty, don't you think?'

'Decidedly. Unless they're visiting a maiden aunt of advanced years, I would say they appear to be casing the joint.'

'And have probably cased several other joints by this time.' The prandial and post-prandial hours in Malvern are soporific. People are either eating or digesting in tranquil somnolence. The occasional car chugged by, but we were the only pedestrians in evidence. A most excellent time for casing. But they wouldn't stand there for ever, and, two minds with but a single thought, we scuttled on hurriedly, casting the occasional glance back to see if we had been observed. We hadn't.

'Of course,' offered Barry on the way back, 'they could have been doing a survey for building repairs, or something.'

'The ferrety one, maybe. But friend Eric is a jeweller – I heard him telling Nora Hilton, and she said, oh, in that case, she wondered if he'd be kind enough to cast a glance over her cultured pearls, because they hadn't been valued in the last twenty years, and she was sure they were worth a fair bit now.'

'And did he?'

'He said he would, if she showed them to him – she didn't have them on. I should say he's a bona fide jeweller all right – but he might be other more questionable things on the side.'

'Now, Dee, let's not start reading too much into this. Unless anyone gets anything stolen, anyway. It's just that we've got nasty suspicious minds. We've no reasonable grounds for suspicion. We'd be better advised to get back on the 'Murder Trail,' pronto.'

'I suppose so.' Somehow I wasn't as enthusiastic about the 'Murder Trail' as Barry. Unlike Stephen Marriner, I couldn't really believe in the characters and situations set up, ingenious though they might be. Barry's ideas in his books are better. And, after the amateur sleuthing we'd done on two separate occasions – well, the real thing is more exciting.

Back at the ranch, or rather, The Hall, Barry parked the Volvo, and we wandered round a bit aimlessly, trying to locate the others. Finally we found them in the 'entertainments room', a large place with several tables and a stage. A game was in progress, based on guessing the values of stated articles in stated years –

e.g. a washing machine in 1959, a pound of butter in 1946, and so on. Nora Hilton's guesses were spot-on, as, surprisingly, were those of another of our two-centre holiday party, David Lydgate, a slim and darkly handsome young civil engineer on leave from Abu Dhabi. Neither of us were very good at the game, though Barry was only a halfpenny off 'a pink suspender belt in 1937'. I wonder how he always knows things like that?

Other games followed, concluding with a mime game based on one popular on the telly, and eventually we dispersed to cudgel our brains again and do any further interrogating, viewing of clues in the 'incident room', etc. Further developments in the 'story' having been fed to us this time by the cast.

'Have you solved all?' I asked Barry.

'Not quite all.' I knew he was a bit worried in case his theories turned out to be completely off-course. After all, it would be a bit of a loss of face for Barry Vaughan, crime-story writer.

'Look at these.' He was unfolding a piece of paper that had been pushed under our door.

'One for you one for me. This says we must write our conclusions, with any relevant comments, plus mentioning any "clues" which were of help to us in reaching said conclusions. And give them in to reception by ten o'clock tomorrow morning.'

'Oh.'

'Well, time for that yet. Come on Dee.' Barry grabbed my arm. 'Let's take Bella for a quick jog – she hasn't been getting much exercise.'

'OK. If we jog past a murder we'll stop and investigate.'

'Naturally. I suppose you'd like the bathroom first when we get back?'

'For that chivalrous offer you may have it first. What's more, I'll scrub your back!'

'Now! Now there's an offer I can't refuse.'

Downstairs, people were drifting round, trying to keep an eye on members of the cast. Feeling, no doubt rightly, that another 'murder' was likely to take place before dinner. As we came back from our jog we were passed by one of the cast, a vivacious character known as 'Veronica', looking very dashing, with long dark hair streaming down the back of her red crepe dress, and wearing very high-heeled red sandals. We watched her make towards the Entertainments Room we'd just left.

'She's done a quick change, hasn't she? I think I'll follow and do a spot of interrogation. After playing hookey earlier, I was getting back in the mood.

'You do that. I'll be soaking in the tub.'

At drinks before dinner the cast circulated again, feeding us further snippets of information and developments in the story-line. Dinner was a cheerful affair, with everyone at our table getting to know the others much better. Mrs Forbes, the Canadian's wife, was wearing a simple turquoise sheath dress and a turquoise and silver choker with matching bracelets which were startlingly exquisite. She conversed intelligently with David Lydgate about the Middle East while Geoffrey Routledge told Karen Margolis about life on the farm. From the expression on Karen's face she found it less than enthralling, which is much what I felt about Ellen rabbiting on about her manager, Jason Purvis, *ad nauseam*. Andrew Forbes found a more sympathetic listener in Nora Hilton, whom he was telling about his haulage business and his family back in B.C. Photos were shown, of Andrew's sons and Nora's daughters, and everyone was getting on swimmingly and enjoying the excellent meal, when Karen Margolis

55

suddenly froze, a forkful half-way to her mouth. Slowly, she put it down on her plate.

'There's something,' she enunciated clearly, 'under this table.' And added, pulling up the tablecloth to investigate underneath. 'It appears to be a body.'

Word spread, and the sheep-like flocking of other guests to our table began. The corpse was 'Veronica', who had a small satisfied smile on her face, though she lay immobile without twitching an eyelash, as if she were aware how striking she must look, with her dark hair fanning out and her perfect complexion against the dramatic red dress. An empty glass lay near her outstretched hand. Obviously, this time the method was poison.

'She must have been there all the time!'

The 'body' was removed, still not twitching a muscle. More babble and exchanging of theories. Any cast members within sight were mobbed and interrogated. No wonder they looked harassed, poor things. Guiltily I remembered Stephen Marriner's request for cigarettes and crisps. I had better slip him at least the former before the night was old.

Barry had his conclusions set down and handed in to reception by nine o'clock the next morning. As a matter of fact, so did I. I hastily wrote my solution over breakfast. From the smug look on Barry's face (he had been rushing round harrying cast members after dinner the night before) I could see that he thought he had the whole thing sewn up. Funny, I'd been the one who was keenest on this holiday, but now, though I was enjoying it, Barry was the more enthusiastic of the two of us and I couldn't summon up the energy to rush round super-sleuthing like some members of the party. Perhaps I was spoilt and blasé when it came to murders, having my very own detective story writer in the home, and some experience of actual sleuthing. Or snooping, as our friend Det. Inspector Ken Graves of the Yard would have put it.

In the event, unsurprisingly, my solution was wrong. In fact, there were various solutions to the various 'murders', explanations of a complexity to baffle Hercule Poirot himself, more than one murderer and some accomplices, and one surprise 'arrest'. I felt a bit down – the way I used to feel after bringing home a school report in which the most glowing remark was 'Diana is trying' – and we all know that can be taken two ways! Barry caught my glum expression and squeezed my hand.

'Cheer up,' he whispered. 'You're good at the real ones.'

'Nobody,' it was declared, 'was correct in every aspect.' Surprise, surprise. 'But some of you did remarkably well. We are awarding a small prize to three people whose deductions were outstandingly good. The first of these is Mrs Nora Hilton.' There was a burst of clapping and Mrs Hilton, dumping her knitting on her neighbour, clambered over knees and handbags and trotted up to the front of the room. More clapping, as she trotted back, flushed and bright-eyed, especially from the more senior of the citizens on the 'Murder Trail'. Always gratifying to show the young ones they don't know it all.

The second recipient was a Scotsman, who had been noticeably active in quizzing cast members, poring over the clues in the 'incident room' and rushing round frenziedly in search of others.

'And finally, Mr Barry Vaughan, who not only made correct deductions and followed clues faithfully, but also provided ingenious comments which have given us ideas for our next plot!' Polite laughter, and Barry went up to collect his trophy.

'What is it?'

'A book token for twelve pounds and a 'Murder Trail

Certificate.' The latter was decorated with a picture of a deerstalker-ed figure peering at a giant fingerprint through a magnifying glass. And lots of gold lettering to the effect that Barry Vaughan had achieved the standards of excellence in sleuthing set by the organisers of 'Murder Trail Weekends.'

'There – you can frame that and put it in your study – just in case anyone doubts your brilliance.'

'Exactly what I intend to do. Hush – more announcements.' But this one was merely to the effect that members of the cast would now be very happy to meet and chat to guests in their *own* characters in the bar.

'This is where the corpses resurrect, of course.' I felt glad I had remembered to pop a packet of cigarettes – *and* a packet of crisps – round Stephen Marriner's door the night before.

Barry got us both orange juices and we joined the admiring group round two senior cast members, who were holding court, and explaining how the whole concept of 'Murder Trail Weekends' came into being. This was fascinating, and the description wound up with the remark, 'We do enjoy doing it, you know, and really get caught up in the "murders"!'

'Veronica', whose real name, we gathered, was Maddy Lang, was saying much the same thing, surrounded by further admiring guests. She was still wearing her red outfit of the night before, tossing back her dark hair and laughing a good deal. From a nearby table 'Edward', alias Stephen, surveyed her ironically. He smiled at me. I smiled back.

'It must have been dreadful keeping still under that table!' someone exclaimed.

'Oh, it was! You've no *idea*! It was really cold, and I got cramps. And then someone moved a leg and put a foot on me. Not on my face, luckily. It was a real effort to stay still and act dead when I was hauled out and carried off. In fact, I'm sure my mouth moved a fraction.' This, I felt, was carrying verisimilitude too far – but of course, although it might seem ludicrous to me, a part is a part, even if it is not *Hamlet*, and part of the job is identifying with it successfully and playing it to the best of one's ability. Veronica had made a reasonably convincing corpse. I remembered I had once, as a student, worked as a waitress in company with a rep. actress who explained that she not only needed to be thoroughly genned up on the job and the daily routine, but she had to *think* like a waitress, to do the job to her own satisfaction. She had certainly got good tips, and I had seen her in a bit-part on television, as a waitress, some years later. No doubt her working experience had stood her in good stead, though she had only been seen clearing off tables and delivering two minutes of dialogue.

I was going to go and chew the fat with Stephen Marriner, looking as if he was glad to have shed the unsympathetic role of the objectionable Edward, but Lissa got there before me. They looked as if they were old friends.

'I am glad you're coming on to Avondale Country Club with me,' Lissa was saying. 'You can give me a hand if the guests get hard to amuse.'

'Delighted – but remember, I'm one of the guests myself.'

'Yes, sir.'

'I need a rest by this time. Not only the telly work but the temperamental fits of Miss Madeleine Lang. I was quite glad to be murdered off to be able to hide in my room!'

'Like Ajax sulking in his tent?'

'Ajax didn't have Maddy Lang dogging his footsteps. If you ask me, he'd never have got anywhere near the

Trojan battlefield if he did. He'd have taken cover long before. Still, I suppose Helen of Troy must have been as much of a nuisance as Maddy Lang, even if she was quieter to have around.'

Guests had begun trickling off. We were, after all, supposed to be checked out of our rooms by now. Lissa stated that the cast would be lunching in the cafeteria, and that any guests who were still around were welcome to join them, if they wished. I joined Barry, who was asking Nora Hilton if she would care for a lift with us.

'No thank you, dear. I'm going to join the cast for lunch, and Lissa Stirling is taking me along later. I think everyone else has a car. Except that nice young man from Abu Dhabi – he left his there. And I think he's going with Miss Margolis. Karen, I mean. They're going to have lunch *en route* and take their time. It is,' she added, with a glance through the window, 'such a lovely day.'

'I think they have the right idea,' Barry remarked. 'Let's follow their example.' We made our adieux to those of the cast we could see, and returned to our room to collect baggage and Bella.

'Right,' Barry declared, heaving the cases in the boot. 'Murder Trail Weekend' over. All corpses back to life. We can now take a rest from sudden death and deductions and give ourselves up to healthy and wholesome pursuits for the rest of the holiday.'

Barry says these things. Only they don't always work out.

Chapter Five

BARRY

Since guests were allowed ample time in transferring from one hotel to the next, and we now had the Volvo, running smoothly and perfectly, we decided to extend our travels, and Bella's, and enjoy the Gloucestershire countryside. It was heavenly weather for it, and we proceeded at a leisurely pace up hill and down green dale, the hedgerows foaming with elderberry blossom and Queen Anne's lace, the meadows sprinkled with buttercups and daisies. Bella gazed out of the back window and uttered appreciative little sniffles. We stopped at Tewkesbury, which I knew but Dee didn't, and after admiring the Abbey, wandered along the charming main street, with its half-timbered houses jutting out over the pavement. Dee bought some attractive flowered place-mats at the National Trust shop, and we lunched in some style at the Hop Pole Hotel, mentioned in *Pickwick Papers*, and, needless to say, endowed with a Pickwick Room and a Pickwick Bar. A kindly waitress took charge of Bella and bore her off to the kitchens for her lunch, while Dee and I speculated on what it must have been like travelling by coach in earlier centuries.

'Picturesque, but I reckon I prefer modern comfort in Hotspur,' Dee finally decided.

'Hotspur?'

'Our doughty charger, the Volvo. I've decided to name him after that swashbuckling character in Shakespeare's Henries.' I didn't protest. Boats may be she's, but to Dee, cars are definitely masculine, and I suppose Hotspur is as good a name as any other for a car. We were deep in discussion of Dickensian characters when the sweets trolley arrived, but after a pause to select (profiteroles for me, strawberries and cream for Dee) I switched the conversation to the historic nature of the area we were in, where the Beauforts were the leading family and there had been more than one battle skirmish.

'In fact,' I pointed out, 'there's an inn further along called The Ancient Grudge.'

'What grudge would that be?'

'Rather an important and long-lasting one – to wit, the Wars of the Roses. The old rivalry between Yorkists and Lancastrians.'

Having paid for our meal and collected a smug-looking Bella, obviously surfeited with all manner of good things, we wandered on, down exquisite little cobbled alleyways where, here and there, tubs of bright blue and red flowers made a colourful splash. Then along the back, by the river path to the old Flour Mills, passing moored cabin cruisers – a family was playing cards in one of them. Tall, narrow, bow-fronted brick houses fronted the water, and along Riverside Walk, dotted with wooden benches and young trees, a duck squawked overhead, green neck outstretched, then swooped down, skimming the water before alighting on it for a swim. Bella scampered up and down, barking a challenge which the duck answered with another derisive squawk.

'Calm down, Bella, and don't get your tootsies wet,' laughed Dee.

'She might enjoy a boat trip,' I suggested brightly. Dee shot me a sceptical look.

'You mean *you* would. Oh well, so would I, come to that. Come on, Bella, we're going on a family outing.'

There was a queue waiting for the longboat, and we managed to get aboard and squash into the last seats before the mooring rope was removed. It was a pleasant, relaxing trip up the Avon, which here runs parallel to the Severn. Up on a hillside was a white, neo-Palladian mansion which turned out to be a home for the elderly. Green grew the rushes on either side, and cruisers with names like *Gypsy, Aquarius, Eliza Doolittle* and *Jaunty Jackaroo* passed us. People waved, and Bella barked a greeting. She's a sociable dog. We were back all too soon at the Tewkesbury Marina, noting this time the block of modern redbrick flats recently constructed by the water and doubtless soon to be sold at high prices, as Dee, her mind temporarily returned to the letting agency, remarked.

'Maybe we should get a cottage in Gloucestershire, for letting,' she remarked wistfully, adding hastily 'when we can afford it, that is.'

'My dear Dee,' I remarked drily, 'it would be a most uncommercial proposition. Anyway, I seem to remember you saying the same thing in Herefordshire. No doubt you'd say the same in Somerset, Wiltshire, Devon, Cornwall or Yorkshire.'

'True,' Dee admitted.

'Failing London,' I went on, 'which is the place *par excellence* for letting, if one can afford the ghastly prices, Kent seems a good bet. Still lots of charming cottagey houses, and it's going to be highly developed, with the Channel Tunnel. Anyway, we're counting our chickens long before they're a gleam in their parents' eyes.'

'Well, a girl can dream, can't she?' There was no answer to that one.

'Now, if you were a food tycoon like Stan Zabrowski . . . '

'I know – there'd be no shortage of country cottages and villas abroad. But then I'd be small, fat and partially bald, instead of the handsome upstanding figure of a man that I am.'

'You may be lacking in millions, but you're certainly not lacking in ego,' Dee retorted crushingly.

'Ah, but you love me with it,' I grinned. 'Come on, sweetness, give us a kiss.' And I wrapped my arms round her in a bear-hug, to the accompaniment of piercing wolf-whistles from a delighted urchin nearby. Bella frisked around our ankles, yapping excitedly. She doesn't like to be left out.

'Oh, get lost, Bella,' Dee exclaimed crossly, as Bella neatly tripped her up. 'Go chase a duck!' She fell back into my receptive arms and Bella obligingly trotted off.

'Sorry, I didn't mean it, Bella,' Dee yelled. 'Come back! Positively *no* ducks, do you hear?' Bella accelerated her pace, and Dee tore off in pursuit. The urchin was now gazing in mingled contempt and pity.

'Mad, quite mad,' his expression said. I can't say I blamed him.

With a mercifully dry Bella retrieved and held firmly in Dee's arms, we sought out a café called The Miss Marple, complete with 1950s-ish Agatha Christie paperbacks in the window, and had a buttered toast and scones tea. Bella flopped over my feet as we sipped our steaming cups, and, inevitably, our thoughts strayed to the Christie-like events of our Christmas holidays the year before, and speculations on what had happened to the assorted guests. The only ones we'd had any news of were the dour and dramatic painter, Morgan Grant, who had had a recent exhibition at an off-Bond Street gallery, and that apparently ill-assorted couple, Gabriel Field and Joyce Bradley, whose lives had turned out so surprisingly well.

'I almost expected a real murder to happen at the fake one, this holiday,' Dee announced, licking clotted cream and jam off her overloaded scone.

'You almost sound disappointed it didn't,' I accused.

'Well, no, of course not. But you must admit, things *happen* when we're around.'

'Agreed,' I said gloomily. 'Like as if we're catalysts, or something. That's what our revered friend Ken Graves of the Yard thinks anyway.'

'I expect,' Dee remarked thoughtfully, 'it comes of you writing crime novels. Sets up vibrations, or something.'

'That's right,' I said bitterly. 'Trust a woman to put the blame on the man!'

'That's an arrantly chauvinist remark,' Dee bristled, her feminist hackles rising. 'I seem to remember a man called Adam who neatly put the blame on a woman called Eve. When they discovered sex – the root of all evil.'

'I thought that was money – or the lack of it.' I held up a peaceable hand. 'Pax, OK?'

'OK.' Dee agreed, after a moment's silent simmer. She started on the toothsome-looking fruit cake and signed for another pot of tea. When it was brought, she settled back for a further gossip.

'But, seriously, Barry. . . '

'Yes, seriously, Dee?' She ignored me.

'Don't you think we've got a motley crowd this time. Rather like the Canterbury Tales.' I digested this remark with a long draught of tea.

'Oh, come, Dee,' I protested. 'They're not in the least like the Canterbury Tales. No Reeve, or Pardoner, or Ploughman, or Knight . . . '

'There's a farmer. And a merchant of sorts – the jeweller. And I suppose the Canadian might be the equivalent of a new-style knight – not the aristocratic type, but he'd probably have been knighted for services to industry if he had been in this country. And the young engineer is a sort of squire type.'

'Hmm. Pretty thin. And positively no Wife of Bath.'

'And the plumber – a Chaucerian artisan . . . No, perhaps not.' She relinquished her literary motif with reluctance. 'Still – a pretty varied bunch, don't you think?'

'Indisputably,' I agreed. 'The Starr girl is pretty gorgeous. Hoping to holiday incognito, but fat chance of that, once you've been on the box. Karen Margolis is stunning, too, but too much of a power-game type for my taste. Mrs Fairclough is a pretty thing, and I have a soft spot for the lissom and lovely Lissa. And Iris Forbes must have been a knockout when she was younger . . . '

'Two,' announced Dee loftily, 'can play at that game. Now I find Andrew Forbes irresistibly masculine. Geoffrey's a sweetie – he makes me feel motherly. David Lydgate is a dream – the epitome of the tall, dark handsome type.'

'And what about Ron and Eric?'

'Well – I wouldn't actually go for Ron Fairclough, but he has a certain sterling British attraction, I suppose.'

'That sounds like damning with faint praise, poor guy. And the estimable Eric, I must admit I don't go for Eric. Too smooth, I don't trust that type an inch or an ell. Too Mac the Knife-ish – the shark has pretty teeth, dear, know what I mean? Mind you,' she added thoughtfully, 'I imagine Forbes has sharkish teeth, too, if he's crossed.'

'And Karen Margolis. Seems common to business types, doesn't it? Or maybe we're being unfair, and thinking in clichés.'

'Maybe.' Dee stirred the remainder of her cooling tea thoughtfully.

'Oh,' she added, 'I forgot to add the extremely personable young actor, Stephen Marriner. *Very* dashing. We've seen him on the box, of course. Remember that enjoyable but rather ridiculous series – *The Baron*? All tavernas and bouzouki music, and cloak and dagger? The one where one expected to see Anthony Quinn doing his Zorba dance at the beginning and the man from MI something at the end?'

'Yes. I think there was a man from MI something somewhere.'

'Probably wolfing down the moussaka. On expenses. I've seen Marriner on the stage, too – yes, I remember; it was Stratford, a few seasons ago. One of the lesser, but not too lesser characters in *Troilus and Cressida*. Very sexy legs, in that tunic. And quite a good actor, too, I got the impression.'

'Dee, your memory is phenomenal. So he's one of those?'

'One of what?'

'A closet Shakespearian.'

'More an out-and-out Shakespearian who's succumbed to the filthy lucre, I expect.'

'Anyway, he doesn't count. We left him behind on the first stage.'

'That's a terrible pun. We didn't, you know – I heard him telling the lovely Lissa that he's coming along for the ride.'

'Or the tennis.'

'Or the sauna.'

'Or the lovely Lissa.'

'Could be. Dee, I think we'd better hit the road.'

'OK. Lead on, Macduff.' I led. Dee followed. Bella, as is her wont, brought up the rear.

*   *   *

We arrived at Avondale Country Club at that lovely summer-evening time when the sun has streaked fading clouds with pale gold and even paler pink, and I brought Hotspur round in a smooth arc down the impressive drive, skirted with green lawn and an occasional tree, round by the rose-bushes in the front. The roses were white and gold and full-blown browny-pink and vermilion. I must gen up on the names of various types sometime. So far, to me a rose is a rose is a rose, and it's not quite good enough. I don't know why the place was called Avondale. Stratford was a good twenty-plus miles away. But I suppose they had to call it something. It was an impressive pile. Your actual manor, long and rambling and built round a square in the middle; Elizabethan Oxfordshire stone, not as honey-pale as Cotswold, with towers and crenellations and what-not. Beside me, Dee gave an appreciative whistle.

'Just so,' I remarked. The other side of the drive, beyond more grassy sward, low greystone buildings decked with rambling roses formed what we were later informed by Lissa were the converted stables – converted into further guest-rooms and a lodge, and alongside those, rather spoiling the general harmony, was a large modern building – the sports centre. Under a topiary archway we glimpsed the pool. It was sizeable and surrounded by chunks of stone – handy for sitting on, if a bit chilly – and Grecian-style pillars. Beyond rolling slopes leading down from the front drive we could catch a glimpse, beyond hedges, of tennis courts. All fairly plush. Dee could catch up on her backhand, which is weak. As is my serve.

'Here we are,' I announced, parking Hotspur with a flourish.

'Woof', agreed Bella approvingly. She had sighted a squirrel nibbling a morsel on one of the grassy swards, and we had to restrain her from going to make its acquaintance.

The inside was nice, too. We took a wander through a baronial hall, draughty, with huge fireplaces and stags' antlers and arquebuses and other weapons on the walls, but discovered that dinner was to be served in a second dining-room, panelled, with lights in sconces and tapestry-weave long curtains at the long Elizabethan windows. The tables were laid with gleaming cutlery and crystal vases of carnations on snowy damask, and it all looked very inviting. We ordered dinner for eight o'clock and were led along corridors by a maid in Edwardian gear, all black and rustling petticoats and frilled apron and cap, to our room. All the rooms had little plaques on them with the names of Kings and Queens of England. Ours was George the Fourth. As we went in, followed by the young man bearing our cases, Ellen Starr issued from Lady Jane Grey, next door. She was wearing slacks and a twinset and stout shoes, and looked all set for a hike through the fields.

'I think,' Dee said, after we had unpacked, 'we should follow Ellen's example, and take a walk. Just to get up an appetite for dinner. We did have rather a lot at lunch and tea. We'd be back in time to bathe and change for dinner. What do you say, Bella?'

'Woof,' Bella endorsed our decision.

We had a nice stroll along a country lane leading upland opposite the hotel. Birds chirruped and there was a cool breeze. Bella rushed around investigating new sights and smells. Really, the energy of that dog makes one feel like an ancient of days. As we returned, we noted two figures coming slantwise across a field. They had some difficulty at a barred gate leading into the lane alongside which appeared to be firmly anchored with wire. Eventually the man vaulted over, and helped the woman to climb precariously over the top. He caught her in his arms as she teetered uncertainly, and set her down gently, releasing his hold reluctantly. The woman was Ellen, and the man, wearing an expression of adoration which could not be mistaken even in the fading light, was Geoffrey Routledge.

'Hi!' Ellen greeted us enthusiastically. Geoffrey's face fell for a moment at having his idyll interrupted by outsiders, but he flushed with pleasure as Ellen tucked her arm through his confidingly.

'Isn't it lovely round here?' Ellen exclaimed. 'So – un-London.' In her musical voice, the trite remark sounded like a pronouncement of one of the Muses. We agreed solemnly that it was, indeed, un-London.

'Not that I've anything against London,' Ellen explained earnestly. 'In fact I love it, and I love my flat at Queens Park – I've been telling Geoffrey all about it, haven't I, Geoffrey?' Geoffrey gave an inarticulate murmur.

'It's just that it's so nice to get away now and then – especially into the country. Maybe I'm just a rustic girl at heart! And Geoffrey's incredibly knowledgeable about farming and country life in general. It's fascinating!' Geoffrey gave another gratified but inarticulate murmur, and I hope Ellen was as sincere as she sounded. The conversation then turned onto Avondale which Geoff had had a chance to explore more thoroughly than late arrivals like us.

'You must go up on the roof – there's a winding stairway all the way up and a fabulous view over to Cheltenham racecourse. And the sports facilities are good.'

'I intend to be a real sporty type while I'm here,' Ellen declared. 'Swimming, tennis, archery – that's something new I'd like to try. And riding. Maybe we could go for a ride tomorrow, Geoffrey?'

70

'I'd love to.'

'I'm not very good, though,' she laughed. 'I'll need a quiet mount, I'm afraid.'

'As long as you enjoy it,' Geoffrey said, his light West-country burr becoming more pronounced with earnestness. 'That's what matters. You needn't worry, I'll look after you.' He made it sound as if he was an Arthurian knight, guarding his lady from vile monsters and dangers of fen and forest.

'Oh, I know you will.' She smiled up at him, confidently.

We'd left it a bit late for our bathe and change, so it was a rush job, with Dee rushing out of the en suite bathroom clad in a towel as I rushed in. Needless to say, the room had all mod cons – mini-bar, telly, hairdryer, trouser-press – the works, as well as being furnished tastefully with blue-and-cream flower-sprigged wallpaper and duvet, wing chairs and pale wood writing desk and breakfast-table. The bathroom was blue, too, but the towels were the usual snowy white. Herbal shampoos and bath lotions abounded. It wasn't Elizabethan, but it was comfortable. The poor old Elizabethans probably had a tin or wooden tub, if that. And rushes on the bare floor, instead of thick-pile wall-to-wall. The only discordant note was the portrait of portly George the Fourth.

'A Hanoverian doesn't seem *quite* . . . ' Dee remarked as she brushed her hair in front of the pale-wood dressing-table. 'Now Richard of Gloucester, much more appropriate.'

'For the area, yes,' I agreed. 'But remember his reputation, Dee. The Princes in the Tower, Lady Anne Neville, Hastings . . . Do you really want him glaring down at us?'

71

'On second thoughts, no. Anyway, I can always imagine Morgan Grant!' And indeed, the artist we had first encountered in Florence, then in Sussex, bore a more than passing resemblance to Olivier in one of his famous roles.

Suitably garbed – Dee in blue-green shot-taffeta, her dark-red hair gleaming burnished, we descended for a Martini in the bar and then dinner. Eric Coventry, I noted, was seated with the Faircloughs. They were half-way through their dinner already. Karen Margolis was with the Forbes. They were on the soup course and talking animatedly. Geoffrey Routledge was partnered with little Mrs Nora Hilton, and obviously trying to make her feel at ease (or it could have been the other way round) while shooting desperately envious glances across the room to the window table where Ellen Starr, resplendent in an embroidered caftan, her abundant dark hair loose around her shoulders and back, was getting on rather more than well with the darkly handsome David Lydgate, to judge from the frequent peals of golden laughter issuing from that quarter.

'Methinks the lady doth laugh too much,' I murmured to Dee, as we canned the menu. A little frown appeared on her face.

'Perhaps. Maybe she's just enjoying herself. I don't think she's trying to make Geoffrey jealous. She's just found another entertaining companion. If you ask me, it's relief at escaping from the Svengali-like Jason, for a while.'

'He does seem to be the dominating influence in her life,' I agreed.

'What are you having, Dee?'

'Oxtail soup, followed by rabbit stew and carrots and broccoli. How about you?'

'Whitebait, followed by pheasant, asparagus and peas, with new potatoes. And perhaps a bottle of Meursault?'

'OK by me. Look – Lissa's on her own over there. Shall we ask her to join us?' But that wasn't necessary, because at that moment a slim reddish-haired figure strode into the room and seated himself at Lissa's table.

'Food!' he declared dramatically. 'Thank heaven! I'm famished.' Stephen Marriner had arrived.

He was not the only late arrival, however, nor the most dramatic. By the time Lissa and Stephen were finishing their main course, and Dee and I had ordered coffee, a vision glided through the door. Dee choked.

'*She was a Gordian shape, of dazzling hue,*' she quoted.

'Keats. Lamia,' I rejoined automatically, being used to Dee's habit of Eng. Lit. quotes.

'But what . . . '

Dee kicked me under the table.

'Observe. Lissa's table.' Obediently, I observed. A vision in a multicoloured slinky gown, red, gold, green, aquamarine, sapphire, sequinned and glittering, her dark hair wound in snaky coils tied with gold thread plaited among the tresses, insinuated herself – there is no other proper word – at the empty chair at Lissa's table.

'Just got here,' she announced. 'Car broke down. Such a bore. Fixed now, though. What's to eat?'

Lissa was looking at her with a little understanding smile. But Stephen Marriner paused, his forkful of fish half-way to his mouth. His handsome face gradually became suffused with red.

'You!' With just such horror a heroine in a nineteenth century melodrama, face with the moustachioed villain, might have pronounced the word.

'What the hell are you doing here?'

Madeleine Lang curved her arm round the back of her chair and leaned back languidly.

'On holiday. Like you. A working girl needs a holiday, you know. Do you mind?'

Stephen's fork clattered to his plate.

'You – you . . . ' I thought he was going to say 'bitch' but he amended it to 'snake'. 'Excuse me, Lissa. Suddenly I don't feel hungry after all. Some things put one off one's appetite.' And he strode out of the dining-room, the very figure of outrage.

There was a silence over the room for a moment. Linda Fairclough gave an audible nervous giggle. Nora Hilton an equally audible 'tut-tut'. Karen Margolis drawled 'So who's upstaged who?' Madeleine Lang shrugged and picked up the menu with every appearance of sangfroid.

'Exactly what I was thinking,' Dee murmured.

Reclining in state in our roomy double-bed that night, we found there was an old 'Thin Man' movie on the telly, and watched it avidly. So did Bella, who became frightfully excited every time the dog Astra appeared on screen.

'She obviously recognises a kindred spirit,' remarked Dee.

'Or a first cousin.' Certainly the two dogs appeared identical.

'I just love those slinky dresses with the shoestring straps,' Dee sighed, half an hour later.

'Obviously, since your nightgown resembles one exactly.' It was a clinging confection of cream silk trimmed with coffee coloured lace. With matching, slightly Empire-style negligée. Very fetching. Very soignée. Very sexy.

'And did I tell you, you were quite the most striking-looking woman in that dining-room tonight?'

'Oh, come on, Barry. What about Ellen? Not to mention the lamia.'

'To other people's eyes, perhaps. Not mine. A redhead in that blue-green number is a knockout to knock out all knockouts. Like that song Sammy Davis Jr. sang in *Porgy and Bess*. You know – the one about a redheaded woman stopping a choo-choo in its tracks.' Dee frowned thoughtfully.

'I don't think it was Sammy Davis Jr. I think I was one of the other characters.'

'Well, the sentiment's the same,' I averred stoutly.

'It's sweet of you anyway, Barry. And to be quite frank, I prefer you to David Lydgate or Stephen Marriner, and you're as goodlooking as either.'

'Thanks, love.' I would have preferred her to say I was *more* goodlooking, but a man can't have everything. And Dee is by nature a truthful girl. Devious when necessary, but basically truthful.

'Can I top you up from the mini-bar?'

'Yes, thanks. More white wine, please.' Bella gave an audible snort. She knows when a couple are gonna get squiffy, a couple are gonna get squiffy. But I don't think she approves. Her diet is strictly non-alcoholic.

Half an hour later, when Nick and Nora (with Asta's help) had just about tied up the mystery, Dee remarked, 'We're as good as they are.'

'Who? Oh – Nick and Nora. Yes, I suppose we are.' I replenished my own glass and remarked casually, 'Who do you think is the prime candidate for murder on this trip?'

Dee looked shocked. 'I thought you didn't like playing this game.'

'No, but since it's not going to happen,' I said comfortably. Dee frowned thoughtfully.

'Well, judging by the scene he made tonight, Stephen Marriner could quite willingly polish off Maddy Lang.'

'Unlikely. I suppose Geoff could go for David Lydgate if Ellen gets too friendly with him.'

'They haven't known each other long enough for the green-eyed monster to develop to that extent.'

'Eric? I'm sure he has a few murky secrets lurking around.'

'Possibly. Or Karen. A rival PR person wants to take over her accounts.'

'And has bribed Nora Hilton to put deadly poison on her knitting needles and stab Karen.' We both chortled at this unlikely picture.'

'Or Andrew Forbes? I bet he's made a few enemies in his time.'

The credits rolled up. Dee went to brush her teeth. I followed suit, switching off the telly on the way back.

'What's the programme tomorrow, Dee?'

'I dunno. Tennis. Maybe riding with Geoff and Ellen.' She sounded drowsy. Bella snored gently at the foot of the bed. I wasn't drowsy. I reached for Dee, and switched off the bedside lamp.

Chapter Six

AN ODD INCIDENT
DEE

As it happened, I didn't get round to the riding till the afternoon. Barry and I (and Bella) woke late and had breakfast in our room, in considerable comfort. That's one of the benefits of being on holiday. We were both drowsy, so I took a shower, first hot, then cold, to wake me up, and set off to investigate the mod cons in the outbuildings. Barry said he'd go for a swim in the pool, and then maybe go for a walk. We arranged to meet at lunch, which apparently was a buffet affair where people wandered in and out at will between twelve and two.

I found David Lydgate, Karen Margolis and Andrew Forbes working out in the gym – or, as it was called, the 'health studio'. This was a truly impressive, spacious place, with a cool air-conditioned breeze circulating and gentle piped music seeping through. The carpet was royal-blue and there were long mirrors the length of one wall. Around were grouped objects of chrome and white plastic tubular structures which might very well have been taken for pieces of modern sculpture or instruments of torture, but were of course the relevant machines – Leg Press, Shoulder Press, Low Pulley, High pulley and so on and so forth. A muscular young man in white, with blond hair, who looked very Norse-God-ish and answered to the name of Norman, was in charge, to see that no one did themselves an injury. David Lydgate was on the Low Pulley, doing 'Bent-Over Rowing'. His face was shiny with sweat. I studied the diagram at the side with interest. It informed me that the major muscle groups affected were the Latissimus Dorsi, Rhomboids, Spinal Erectors and something else Major and Minor.

'Having fun?' I asked.

'You could call it that,' he panted. 'By the way,' – I waited while he grunted and gasped for enough breath to finish – 'you're meant to book the machines in advance.'

'Oh, I expect Norm will overlook that and fit her in,' Karen called. You will, won't you, Norm?' Norm cast her an admiring glance. She was dressed in ice-blue leotard and tights which showed off her splendid figure, and was doing something complicated with the High Pulley, kneeling on the floor and pulling the bar behind her head. I noted her streamlined thighs and flat stomach with envy.

'Of course. Which machine would you like?' I elected for sit-ups on a white plastic bed with plastic bumps for the knees to go over and rollers to put ones insteps under. Good for the tum. Afterwards I might go for the Vertical Chest (Butterfly), which was good for the pectorals (Major and Minor). I didn't think Karen would quarrel with me over it. Her pectorals were obviously in absolutely no need of development. In the centre of the room Andrew Forbes was peddling away energetically on the Aerobic Bicycle.

'Isn't your wife going to work out with you?' I asked him – my machine being just behind his and close enough for conversation.

'Iris? No. She doesn't need to, really – she's in terrific condition. Comes of having been a nurse, I suppose; they're always conscious of keeping the body in trim.' I agreed that Iris certainly looked in marvellous shape.

'She's out riding, I think. Started with a few lengths in the pool before breakfast, and some jogging. Said she might look in here later in the day.'

'You think she'll have the energy, by that time?'

'Oh, I expect so. Anyway, she might just want to use the other facilities.' He nodded his head to a door at the side. 'Down that corridor there are the saunas and the sunbeds. The sunbeds are rather luxurious – upholstered in red plush, like banquettes in Edwardian-style pubs. And further along there's another building with a balcony restaurant overlooking a jacuzzi. Just a tea-and-coffee place really, with a small bar for those who want to sip a Martini and gaze down through a trellis screen at the more active splashing round below.'

'It's certainly a well-equipped place.'

'And well-designed, so it's not too much of an eyesore against the background of the Elizabethan part,' David chipped in. He had finished his rowing exercises and had moved to the Leg Press, but was taking a breather in between.

'The building near the pool contains the squash and billiards rooms, and leads into this wing, which goes up to within a few yards of the jacuzzi building, on a square, the fourth side being made up of the Elizabethan cottage block which contains the outside bedrooms and screens the rest, a very pretty lawn with flowerbeds and a gravelled walk round the edge forming the centre.' I remembered he was a civil engineer, used to the layout of buildings and looking at architectural designs. I suppose they develop a visual sense.

'Has Barry gone riding, too?' called Karen, who had

been chatting cosily with Norm while continuing her exercises. She must have been very fit indeed – it didn't seem even to disturb her breathing.

'No. He's at the pool. Unless he's gone back to sleep! Anyway, we don't know yet where to find the horses!'

'Out of the hotel grounds, along the main road, turn left, then right and straight ahead for a while and you'll see the notice for the riding school. You have to pay extra, at the school, of course.'

You sound as if you've been there before. Have you stayed here before?'

No – but I asked the way at reception, and the girl drew me a little map on the back of an envelope. Anyway, I've got a good memory for directions. Norm, I think I'll transfer to the Low Pulley David was on. And that'll do me for today. I'll have a go on a sunbed then, and maybe a dip in the pool. Dee, do you fancy riding this afternoon?'

'I'd love to,' I said, 'but I can't answer for Barry.'

'Never mind Barry. Husbands and wives don't have to stick together all the time on holiday. What about you two?'

David said he'd like to go, but Andrew refused politely.

'Norm?' The young man shook his head ruefully.

'I have to be on duty here.'

'Of course. What a pity. Maybe another time, when you're free.'

'Delighted.'

I removed my hands from behind my head and my feet from under the roller, and hobbled towards the Chest Press. Karen laughed.

'Never mind, Dee, it's always worst the first day. Don't do too much, though, or you'll be too painful to go riding later.' She was right, of course. At any rate, my velour jogging suit concealed the worst of my bulges, so I didn't look too bad. Barry's always very flattering about my curves, but I am a stone overweight. Though with all the unremitting physical activity round Avondale Country Club, with any luck I'll have shed it by the time we leave.

David and Karen went off to the sunbeds, Andrew transferred to one of the machines, supervised by Norm, and I wended my painful way to the saunas. After sweating it out in the heat, with a luxurious shower to follow, I was beginning to feel much better. Quite fit, in fact, and starting to get peckish. I went to round up Barry from the pool. He was floating at the shallow end, looking pensive. Bella, shaking wet drops all round her vicinity, was playing with a couple of children. They, and some adults I did not recognise, were regular Country Club members, not necessarily staying at the hotel, but who motored in to use the facilities, especially the pool and the bar in the clubhouse, though the squash rooms were popular too.

All this I gathered from Barry, who had been socialising. Ellen and Geoffrey were in the pool too, so they had obviously not gone riding after all. The former was looking fetching in a black and white one-piece Lycra swimsuit. Nora Hilton was sitting at the poolside with a pink towelling robe over her swimsuit. She had a paperback of *The Murder of Roger Ackroyd* face down on the ground, and was engaged with the ubiquitous pink knitting. Maddy Lang, in scarlet bikini, ran out to the edge of the diving board, her tanned body spectacularly streamlined and slim, and jacknifed effortlessly in a perfect dive. One of the Country Club men whistled, and there was a short burst of clapping.

'The epitome of chic', Barry remarked.

Maddy reminded *me* of a rather beautiful but truculent black cat. I wondered idly where the Faircloughs were.

'Out riding. So's your Stephen Marriner – he made off with Lissa. So he's missing Maddy's exhibition!'

'Or her exhibitionism,' I murmured. Pity she couldn't latch onto David Lydgate instead. But Karen seemed to have him in her sights. Though she had seemed more than passing interest in the gorgeous Norm. Perhaps Norm would take a shine to Maddy and vice versa, and then everybody would be paired up nicely. I mentioned that Iris Forbes was riding as well, and that I would be going with Karen and David that afternoon. As I had surmised, Barry did not appear interested in either riding or the strenuous joys of the health studio.

'I think I'll take a gentle stroll and then use the sunbed after lunch,' he decided. Barry likes to lead into his exercise gradually. He's a doggy-paddle man rather than a fast-crawl one, metaphorically speaking. 'And maybe discuss the art of the detective story with Nora. I've been angling for a date for the past half-hour.'

'You should be so lucky. She'll probably be charging round the tennis court with Eric Coventry. Or practising archery on the range. If she's a health and fitness fiend like everyone else round here. It's a bit like that ad on the van that goes round Woodfield. You know – the one with a large picture of Sylvester Stallone displaying his biceps and the words "'Are you overweight, out of condition? Gym'll Fix It. Come to Flexibody. Studio opposite Patel's Minimarket".'

'I always thought Sylvester Stallone was over-rated.' And it's true that for a man whose pursuits are so largely sedentary and who likes his food, Barry has a good figure. He says his brain energy consumption burns up the calories, which may be true. One does, of course, have to remember that he's a secret Saturday-morning jogger, when he does his 'Loneliness of the Long-Distance Runner' bit at six ack emma round the park, back in time to shower and bring out the orange juice and toast before I set off for, the supermarket, and all the other necessary Saturday calls.

There seemed to be a general drift towards changing rooms just then. I collected Bella and we ambled towards the hotel. Lunchwards. Barry could catch us up if he was ultra-quick. Which he wasn't. I collected a salad platter, wholemeal rolls and cheese and a glass of white wine. Beside me, Iris Forbes was trying to make a choice. She was still dressed in jodhpurs and white shirt, and looked like a *Vogue* picture of the chateleine of a stately home.

'I'm afraid I haven't changed yet,' she said. 'Just washed my hands and rushed in here. All that fresh air gets to the appetite. I just couldn't wait a moment longer!'

'Oh, don't apologise. When a girl's gotta eat, a girl's gotta eat. I know the feeling so well. Can I pour you some wine?' Across the table, Geoffrey Routledge was spreading pâté on French bread for Ellen Starr, who was continuing some saga started as they walked across from the changing rooms.

'So you see, classical music isn't my thing, though I love it. I feel a bit guilty in a way, because my mother was a gifted pianist. In fact she had a lot of professional success and played at the Leeds Festival and the Wigmore Hall and all over, really. Jeannette Stark, her name was. That's why I took the stage name "Starr". It's like Stark, without being identical.'

'And, of course, the connotations of being a star', Geoffrey suggested.

'That too. It's clever of you to think of that straight off. But then you are, aren't you, Geoff. Cleverer than you seem. Oh dear, that sounds insulting. I mean, you notice things other people don't. Like Madeleine Lang being left-handed. I hope we have a good ride this afternoon. Pity we missed out this morning, but the pool was so inviting! Poor old Jason – he'd love it here. Now, I'm still going to have the quietest mount, mind!'

A widening stain of wine spread itself over the table-cloth. Iris Forbes looked at it ruefully.

'There goes my drink! Did I spill it or did you or someone else? Never mind – at least it isn't red.' She took the bottle and gave herself a refill.

'Shall we sit down over there? Your husband's just come in, but he seems to have been nobbled by Miss Lang. Mine seems to have disappeared off the face of the earth!'

'He's probably still under the sunbed.' I told her about the health studio activities, and asked her about her nursing career. Some of her anecdotes proved very interesting, and I was sorry to have to break off and excuse myself to get changed. My velour tracksuit was not quite the best garb for horse-riding. Iris was consuming fruit salad when I left her. She glanced a bit anxiously at her watch and I wondered what her programme was for the afternoon. Probably she'd round up her missing husband for a swimming marathon. From what he'd said, she was the hyperactive type.

I hadn't brought jodhpurs, but found a shirt and pair of slacks that seemed to fit the bill, with lace-up shoes which gave a good grip. I tied my hair back with a ribbon. No hard hat, so I'd just have to hope I didn't come a cropper. Ellen was going into Lady Jane Grey as I emerged from George the Fourth.

'Oh, Dee, you look really dashing! Do wait for me – I'll change quickly, promise!'

'OK.' I positioned myself beside the window and gazed out. Iris Forbes was walking round the building towards the main gate. She had a beige raincoat over the jodhpurs. I squinted at the sky. It was definitely cooler than this morning. I hoped the weather wasn't breaking. Karen Margolis came out from the reception area. She was wearing jodhpurs and a black riding hat, and looked fantastic. David Lydgate was with her. He was in jeans and denim shirt, and was dashingly cowboyish. They looked up in the direction of my bedroom area, and conferred. I leaned out.

'Hi!' I shouted. 'Be down soon. Wait!'

'OK. Don't be too long.' I knocked on Ellen's door.

'Ellen, haven't you changed yet?'

'Just coming!' came the muffled response. A minute later the door opened and Ellen emerged. She was in a black velvet suit, which looked terrific, with a white polo-neck acrylic jumper. But not the most comfortable or coolest gear for riding, surely. Still – ours not to wonder why. I forbore comment, just looking pointedly at my watch.

'I know – sorry, Dee. Listen, be an angel, and wait while I pick up Geoff. He's in Richard II, one of the outside bedrooms.'

'All right,' I sighed. 'I'll see you at the main gate. If I can prevail on Karen and David to wait there with me.'

As it happened, we were delayed still further, as a slim figure in blue jeans and scarlet shirt came running round from the back of the hotel, calling, 'Wait for me!' It seemed to be the general *cri de coeur*.

'Maddy Lang. Red seems to be her colour.' Everyone waited.

I suppose there was no great earth-shaking hurry. Karen said she'd got the desk to ring the riding-school and reserve us some mounts, including a couple of quiet ones. In the absence of Lissa, she was taking charge. The Maggie Thatcher of Covent Garden. Well, I suppose someone

85

had to be at the helm. As it happened, we stopped off for a drink at a pub anyway.

As we turned off into the side road, we encountered Stephen and Lissa, both be-jeaned and flushed and sweaty. They had their arms linked, and looked happy.

'Hail, blithe spirits,' Stephen greeted us, with a flourish. Enjoy your afternoon's sport with that noble animal, the horse. Me, I have discovered that the proper study of mankind is woman.' And he squeezed Lissa's arm.

'Pay no attention,' she told us. 'He's an actor. They tend to talk in irrelevant quotations.' The pair passed on, and Maddy made a small sound. She looked, suddenly, rather lost and woeful. David Lydgate dropped back and fell into step beside her.

'Have you done much riding, Maddy?' he asked. A kind young man.

'No. Well, yes. I mean, I've had lessons and all that, but though I enjoy it I'm not very good. I need a quiet, steady mount or I'm terrified!'

'There you are.' Karen was triumphant. 'I knew we'd need at least two quiet horses. I hope,' she added ominously, 'no one else is scared.' Silence. I doubt if anyone would have dared declare it even if we were

'Good.' David was now chatting, in a low voice, to Maddy. Ellen fell into step beside me and Geoff moved up to accompany Karen. Large and attractive houses of various styles lined one side of the road. On the other, green meadows extended outwards and downwards. The sun came out again. It was a peaceful scene. Another five minutes' walk and we came across the 'Cheltenham Riding School' notice, and an arrow leading up a small lane. Not that we were anywhere very near Cheltenham, really, but I suppose with the racecourse within view from the heights, you couldn't blame them. Karen introduced our party, and insisted again on the need for quiet mounts for Ellen and Maddy.

'Of course. Snuggles and Morning Star. They're both lovely quiet horses. Very friendly. Just give them a couple of pats and you're their friend for life.' The weatherbeaten middle-aged woman led out two white horses with grey flecks. They looked identical, except that Snuggles, Maddy's mount, was fatter and stood there passively while Morning Star snickered and nuzzled Ellen, who responded with a nervous pat.

'That's right, love,' Geoffrey encouraged. 'Just show her you're not afraid.' He helped Ellen to mount, and showed her how to hold the reins properly, before mounting his own horse, a tall bay, and drawing it up beside her. The rest of us were suitably mounted, and the weatherbeaten woman clattered to our head.

'I'm Frieda. Now we're going down the lane and into an open field, and then across these downs. First a trot, then a canter, and if you feel up to it, a gallop on the final stage. I'll tell you when it's time to turn back, so don't worry about that. Now remember, don't pull hard on the reins. It pulls at the horse's mouth and it's not necessary. I'll be riding alongside you, and so will Tom here, and if anyone's in difficulties we'll be there to help. They're lovely horses, all of them, and they enjoy a good run. Prince, the bay, can be a little bit tricky, but he's a lovely horse too. Now just follow me; a quiet little trot to start with.'

My horse, a black one with a white blaze, called Satan, proved a bit frisky. Geoffrey kept Prince reined in firmly so he could stay beside Ellen, though I guessed they'd probably get separated later in the gallop. Beside me, Maddy's mount, Snuggles, was worrying me. He kept shaking his head and rolling his eyes. Maddy tried to soothe him, but without much success. She was looking worried, too, but coping better than Ellen. I decided she was probably perfectly competent on a horse, and that she had decided to play the helpless little woman role for a change – possibly in competition with Ellen. We turned into a field and, at the instructors' directions, the trotting was gradually changed to a canter. Geoffrey was still sticking close to Ellen, who still looked nervous. She had the kind of smile on that people put on when they are trying to prove they are *not* nervous. David, I noted, had a perfect seat on his horse. He seemed more cowboylike than ever – very dashing. Maddy and Snuggles were ahead of me now. Snuggles was rearing his neck and showing his teeth, and trying to break into a gallop. Maddy was having a job to hold him in.

'If that's a quiet horse, give me Satan,' I thought. My own mount was going like a dream. I wondered momentarily if Maddy could have been given the wrong mount, but that didn't seem possible. Frieda obviously knew all the horses well.

We were going down an incline now, a gradual one leading to a couple of clumps of tree with a space in between. The horses were manoeuvred closer together to go through the space. Suddenly there was an outraged whinny from Maddy's horse, which broke away and broke into a fast galllop.

'Hey! Too early!' came Frieda's authoritative tones, coloured with annoyance. 'Rein him in!' But it was too late for that. Maddy was completely out of control, one of the reins out of her hand and dangling. She held onto the other rein with the other, and made a grab for Snuggles' main with the free hand. A quick, terrified look back over her shoulder revealed a white blur of a face. Snuggles galloped on madly, the Billy Bunter of the equine class suddenly transformed into a demon. Galloping hooves thundered past me as Geoffrey left Ellen's side and galloped to the rescue, catching up with David, who was doing the same thing. Satan, not to be left out, speeded up his pace, and, ignoring my efforts to hold him back, moved outwards to the side, so that the three of us thundered down practically abreast. Snuggles was now making for the space between the trees and Maddy had started yelling. To my horror, she suddenly seemed to lift from the horse's back – she had already lost her stirrups some time gone – and stay suspended for an instant as Snuggles galloped on regardless without her, then fall heavily into a crumpled mass on the ground. There were cries and shouts from our party. David reached Maddy first, and reined in his horse expertly, sliding off and running to Maddy's prone form. The scarlet shirt made a bright streak on the grass. Geoff, on the huge bay, had set off in pursuit of the runaway horse. I reined in Satan with difficulty. I didn't get off, fearing that Satan might take it into his head to go off in pursuit of the bay and Snuggles.

'Is she OK?' I asked David, who was gently prodding the silent figure.

'I think so, except that she's fainted, and there will be bruising. Nothing seems to be broken. I can't make out how she came off like that. It was weird – almost as if she'd been grabbed by an unseen hand.' Satan became impatient and wandered off to a clump of trees. Something caught my eye and I inspected. And did a double-take.

'In a sense, she had,' I commented grimly. 'David, will you look at the trees in that other clump and see if you can see some greenish-grey wool tied onto one of them.'

'What on earth . . . ?' But he obeyed. The others were pounding up to us now, and in the distance I could see Geoff trotting back slowly, with a captive and now docile Snuggles.

'Well?'

'Yes, there is. A few strands, sort of loosely plaited together at intervals. Quite long, and broken off. You mean . . . ' He wasn't slow in catching on, even if he did speak in clichés.

'The matching strand is my side. Come and check – then we'll both have witnessed it.'

Tom, the second instructor, had dismounted, and was clucking over Maddy, who in true story-book princess fashion, now came awake gradually and sat up gracefully. She didn't exclaim in wonder 'Where am I?' but that was all that was missing. I was amused. Obviously she was feeling recovered enough to put on a bit of a show. Everyone gathered round, full of solicitude.

'I'm all right,' Maddy declared bravely, then winced and rubbed herself ruefully as she moved. Tom helped her, gingerly, to her feet.

'But I'm not getting on that damned horse again. I thought you said it was quiet and sweet-tempered!' she rounded on Frieda. 'If that's a quiet horse I'd hate to get one of the others. I might have been killed!'

'Snuggles is quiet!' Frieda glared at her. 'I don't know what you did to him. You must have been pulling cruelly on the reins.'

'I was not! The reins were quite loose, as a matter of fact.'

'Yes, they were,' I confirmed. 'At least, when she was riding beside me, and as far as I could see, the rest of the time. Maddy, when you fell off. Did you feel anything obstructing you? Like a length of twine, holding you back?'

'Yes – now that you mention it, I did. You mean someone tied string onto the trees?'

'Not string, wool. Different strands, loosely knotted together. Weak enough to break, but strong enough to hold you back for as long as it took for Snuggles to gallop on without you, and high enough to obstruct you, but not him. If your feet had still been in the stirrups they'd almost certainly have slipped out at that point. Look for yourself.'

Maddy hobbled over and did as I suggested. So did Frieda. David demonstrated the other end of the wool trap, and showed the break, at the other tree. Maddy's voice rose in fury.

'Someone did it on purpose! What a bloody nasty trick!'

'We don't know that,' David put in pacifically. It could have been kids playing.' Maddy snorted sceptically. It was at this point that we were rejoined by Geoff, leading a chastened Snuggles by the reins. His friendly, open face looked grim. Snuggles rolled his eyes. Foam flecked him. He was not a happy gee-gee.

'I examined this horse,' Geoff said accusingly. 'And I found this under his saddle. No wonder the poor animal bolted. It was rubbing his skin raw and digging into him. It must have been driving him mad.' He held out his open palm. More manoeuvring of horses from those still mounted, to look.

'This' was a large, prickly burr. I could see that every movement Maddy made on the saddle would have increased the painful irritation it produced. After a bit it would have been unbearable.

'Who saddled this horse?' Geoff demanded. An obvious lover of animals, he sounded like the Grand Inquisitor. This new, masterful, man-of-action stance wasn't doing him any harm with Ellen, one could tell from the expression on her face.

'I did.' Tom spoke, his nut-brown face defensive. 'And I can tell you that thing wasn't there then. Right as rain, he was.'

'When did you saddle him?'

91

'At lunch-time, ready for the afternoon ride. He'd been out for a run this morning, a local kid that always rides him. That was with a couple of other kids and their mum and the group from your hotel. Then he had a rub-down and a rest and his dinner, and another rest, then I saddled him for the afternoon ride. I use Snuggles a lot, because there's always a demand for a quiet horse. Nearly always, anyway. From someone.'

'So you'd always use Snuggles in preference to, say, Morning Star?' I asked.

'Yeah. As long as he was well and hadn't been overdoing it. We don't overtire him, you know. He gets plenty of rest.' The defensive tone was back.

'Sure. We can see he's well-cared for,' I replied soothingly. Certainly the plump little horse didn't look as if he was run into the ground. Geoff was now stroking him and making soothing noises, and, with the dread prickly object removed, he was responding. Karen Margolis stared at me curiously.

'So what's with you, Dee? I mean, why all the questions?'

'My naturally curious nature.' I tried to laugh it off. 'Poor old Snuggles. It was a nasty trick all right.

'Children can be diabolical. Especially these days.'

It was an explanation everyone seemed happy to fall in with, for the moment anyway. The alternatives being too complicated and mind-boggling. True, Maddy snorted again and demanded, 'Poor old Snuggles? What about poor old Maddy? I've had a very nasty experience. And how am I going to get back, I'd like to know? I positively refuse to go anywhere with that animal again.'

Frieda appeared reluctantly to realise she had a genuine grievance. 'We've got a jeep. If you stay here Tom will bring it down. There's a gate into the road a hundred yards or so further down the field.'

'I'll stay with you,' David offered, doing his parfit gentle knight bit. 'I can ride to the school afterwards.'

'Thanks.' She shot him a grateful look.

The rest of us made our way back at a canter, except for Tom, who took over Snuggles' reins from Geoff and trotted decorously behind leading him. It cannot go down in history as a successful ride. Geoff looked down-at-mouth, as one who has just discovered he had brought the bad news from Aix to Ghent. I wondered if Maddy and David would improve the shining hour by discussing the wool trap and the prickly burr, and end by concluding that the two were connected and that someone meant Maddy considerable harm. She would hardly have broken her neck, though I suppose it was not impossible, but she could have broken a leg, an arm, or a collarbone. And the whole thing must have been carefully set up; the wool rope planted and the prickly burr not too long before we arrived for the afternoon rota. Of course, it could have been slipped under Snuggles' saddle by one of our party, but that seemed unlikely. Again, the two incidents might be unconnected. In which case either it was a malicious prank, as I had suggested to calm things down, and the wool rope was the residue of some kid's game, which they hadn't thought to remove. Or the wool had been placed with evil intent, but indiscriminately against whoever arrived at the trees first, or against someone who seemed the most likely first arrival. No – it was all, as the King of Siam said to Anna, 'a puzzlement', and rather too much for me. I'd try it out on Barry.

Chapter Seven

BARRY

While Dee was off riding, I sneaked off to the health studio and had a go on a couple of the machines under the aegis of Norm. I was joined by Stephen Marriner, who seemed considerably more at home on the machines than I was, in spite of the fact that he was pleasantly and mildly tipsy.

'Just drank my lunch,' he explained. 'Now gonna work it off.' We adjourned in due course to the saunas, where, from adjoining sauna cubicles, we chatted about this and that. Largely about Stephen's appearances as Adam Derwent in Corfu, which was interesting, and about the televising of my spoofy crime novels, *Penny for the Guy et al.*, which had brought me into brief contact with camera crews, location shooting, continuity girls and the whole shebang, on the rare occasions when I was allowed a look-in on the action. Stephen wanted to know more about Dee, for whom he had formed a liking for, and went on at some length about Lissa – how restful and calming she was, how efficiently organised, how unlike the general run of women he met, etc., etc. By this time we'd adjourned to the sunbeds, which one operated oneself, by coins in a slot. Norm had closed up shop, since it didn't look likely anyone else would be along for a workout. I lay there lazily, with Stephen's voice washing over me, and started to drowse. Meanderings about the beloved tend to be of monumental boredom except to the one who is uttering them. To change the subject, I asked, 'Did you enjoy your ride?'

'Eh? Oh, ride. Before lunch. Yes, it was OK.'

'What are the horses like?'

'Much as you might expect. Rather better, actually. There was a spirited number called Satan – a bit much for little Linda Fairclough to handle, so they put her on a mare of quieter disposition. That held us up. My horse was fine – went really fast on the gallop. Lissa got stuck with a fat'n'lazy creature called Snuggles. I gather he usually gets given to the children. Iris Forbes was the surprise element! She had a huge bay monster, Sultan, to handle, and proved the most superb horsewoman! Fantastic! I can see what millionaire Forbes saw in her.'

'Is he really a millionaire?'

'Is he ever! That guy is rich like you and I dream of rich, Vaughan.' There was a gusty sigh.

'You're doing all right with your "Baron" role. In no time at all you'll be in the supertax class.'

'Yeah. Well, I was lucky the pilot series took off all right. Still – easy come, easy go, in our profession. You're everyone's baby one year; the next, you're old-hat or some scandal or other has toppled you. Or the play folds. Or something.'

'I wouldn't have thought scandal was a big problem. Especially in this day and age.'

'No – well, you'd be surprised. Still, I'm not a bigamist or a multiple murderer, so maybe I'll be OK.' I waited for further revelations, but they didn't come, and he got back onto the topic of Lissa again. I sighed, and made appropriate noises at appropriate moments.

'I must do this more often,' I announced, as we

emerged from the building some time later. 'I feel fantastic.'

'The new you. Bet Dee will encourage you. Speaking of which, there is the lady. Why don't you join me for a drink on the terrace?' I agreed, and looked with interest at the figure of Geoffrey Routledge, stalking by grimly, still in his riding gear.

'Geoffrey Routledge looks like J.R. Rides Again . . . and Again . . . ' I commented to Dee, when we were installed on the terrace sipping iced drinks. Dee had ordered a Mint Julep in Gloucestershire. She settled for a Harvey Wallbanger.

'Yes, well . . . he's got reason.' I sighed. Dee occasionally has what I call 'a touch of the enigmatics'. She now started quizzing Stephen about his ride before lunch. He seemed a bit puzzled, as well he might, and started to look peeved when she got onto his relationship with Madeleine Lang.

'Really, Dee, do I have to discuss Maddy? Look, she's not a bad kid in her way, just spoilt. And I admit she's very attractive. It's just that she seems to rub me up the wrong way. Deliberately, at times, if you ask me.'

'Well, for your information, Stephen, Maddy had an accident this afternoon. And it could have been very nasty indeed.'

'Is she all right?'

'Apart from shock and bruises, yes. The point is, this particular accident seemed to have been engineered deliberately.'

'Oh!' Stephen digested this for a moment, then light dawned. 'And you mean I don't like her, so I did it? Dee, that's grossly unfair. For your information, it's not my style to go round injuring young women who just happen to be irritating to me. That kind of thing went out with the Borgias.'

'Calm down.' Dee put a placating hand over his. 'The point is, you had opportunity. The means were easy enough to get hold of. And you seem to have a motive of a kind. But I agree – the motive is far too insubstantial.'

'Thank you for those few kind words.' Stephen was still flushed angrily. 'What happened, anyway?'

Dee outlined the recent happenings for us. It certainly seemed very odd.

'Where is she now?'

'Down by the tennis court, watching a game.' Stephen pushed his chair back, and drained his drink.

'Then if you'll excuse me, I think I'll go to pay my condolences. It might,' he added with a wry smile, 'be a good time to proffer the olive branch. All this bickering gets wearying.'

'That could,' remarked Dee thoughtfully, as he departed, 'be a very clever young man.'

'Smoke screen, you mean?'

'Yes. He's right – this Kate and Petruchio act is too ridiculous to be taken seriously as a motive. Which anyone with any sense would see. But there might be an underlying motive.'

'Wheels within wheels, and all that jazz?'

'Quite so, my dear Watson.'

'I suppose she could be blackmailing him. He made a couple of odd remarks about scandal.' I expounded.

'Interesting. Then, of course, Maddy Lang is a wealthy girl in her own right – or will be. I gather.'

'Is she?'

'Yes. Lang's construction, granddaddy. Lang's fast-food franchise, uncle.'

'Oh.'

'So someone might want to bump her off, to get her share of the loot. Someone with some connection with her or who has hired someone here.'

'Go over anything you told me before. From lunchtime.'
Dee sighed gustily and raised her eyes to heaven, but
complied.

'That deserves another drink.' I ordered another Harvey
Wallbanger and a plain Rose's lime juice for myself.
Having sweated off some weight (I confidently hoped),
I didn't want to put it right back on with alcohol.

'There's another possibility, Dee. Anyone who was
within earshot of Ellen Starr during lunch and probably
before lunch too could have heard her say she required
a quiet mount. Maddy's intention to join the ride
doesn't seem to have been as well publicised. You
say Karen ordered a couple of quiet horses, but that
was just Karen's high-handedness – or wisdom. As far
as anyone else was concerned, until Maddy came out
with her nervousness with horses, there was only one
nervous and inexperienced rider. And Snuggles was the
horse always allocated to children and the inexperienced.
Morning Star was second choice.'

'You mean, Ellen could have been the target, and it
was just chance that Ellen got Morning Star and Maddy
got Snuggles.'

'Precisely. On the other hand, as you point out, the
burr stuck under Snuggles' saddle might well have been
the work of a child – it's a childish thing to do, unless
deliberately aimed to produce the effect it in fact had.
And the wool rope could have been aimed at anyone on
the ride.'

'So we're back to square one.'

'I'm afraid so,' I said. 'The only thing we can do is
keep a wary eye on both Maddy and Ellen, just in case.
Let's drop the subject just now and go and watch the
tennis 'till dinner.

Stephen found Maddy watching the Faircloughs play Eric

Coventry and Karen Margolis at tennis. She was sitting alone, looking forlorn. He marched up and plonked himself down at her side.

'Maddy, do you think I set up that riding accident to hurt you?'

She looked startled, swinging round to face him.

'I – no, of course not. That's stupid. Why would you do a thing like that?'

'Search me.'

'I mean, I know you don't like me, but you don't *hate* me – do you? Stephen?'

'You're too lightweight to hate. No, of course I don't. I think you're spoilt, full of your own importance, a bit of a bitch and a pain in the ass, and I'm fed up with you dogging my footsteps, but, no, I don't hate you. Hate is reserved for people who have done one some unforgivable injury or caused one considerable suffering. You, my dear Maddy, do not come into that category. Nor have you threatened me – except with your continued presence – nor attempted to ruin me, nor aroused the green-eyed monster. In fact, if you were less of a pain and kept a lower profile we might even be friends.' There was a long pause. Maddy looked on the verge of tears.

'Boy, you really know how to make a girl feel good,' she ventured in a wavery voice at last. 'OK, as from now you've achieved your objective. I've stopped fancying you and I'll stop trying to get your attention. You can have Lissa or whoever you want, and I won't interfere.'

Stephen took her arm and gave it a little squeeze.

'Then that's settled, we can get off our battling-gear and start to be buddies. Sit with me at dinner tonight, for starters. If we talk to each other rationally we'll probably find a good deal to like in each other. I think you've the makings of a very good actress, by the way.'

'Thanks.' Maddy looked gratified.

'And, much as I hate to introduce the subject again, if someone is gunning for you, I think I'd better take up bodyguard duties. We thespians have to stick together, you know!'

Iris Forbes removed her clothes and left them in a neat pile on top of her sandals. She left them outside the sauna cubicle, on the floor. Checking the temperature thermostat, she wrapped the huge fluffy white towel, left on the wooden shelf, around her, and poured water from a beaker onto the coals. It sizzled and hissed. Iris read a couple of pages of her book, and hummed along with the canned music which permeated all parts of the outbuilding. At that moment 'It Was Just One of Those Things' was being played. She slipped out, adjusted the thermostat again, was very careful pulling the door to. Off came the towel, and she ranged her lean, suntanned body along the wooden shelf. She stifled a yawn. It would be so easy to drop off to sleep, now, after her action-packed day. And with the music playing, she wouldn't hear anyone outside the cubicle, if they were careful to be quiet . . .

BARRY

We were dressing for dinner when I discovered my watch was missing.

'Damn!' Dee looked round from the dressing-table, where she was fastening on earrings.

'What's the matter?'

'I've left my watch in the other block. Sauna or sunbed room, I think.'

'Maybe someone's handed it in at the desk.'

'I doubt it. I think Stephen and I were the last customers of the day. No, I'd better go over and get it. Order the first course for me, will you, darling? Soup, if it sounds decent. Otherwise, whatever you think I'd like.'

'All right. You might catch me up before I go into the dining-room, anyway, because remember I have to take Bella along for her dinner.'

It was still light, but there was something a little eerie about the empty outbuildings. I went first to the sunbed area, and to my relief found the watch on the ground beside it. It's a serviceable Rolex, a present from Dee. Women cut up rough if you lose their presents. Besides, I was attached to it. Coming out into the corridor, through the health studio, I nearly bumped into a slim figure with a light flowery fragrance drifting about it.

'Oh, hello, Lissa. What are you doing here? Rounding up stray sheep?'

'Something like that. Iris Forbes came over for an evening session in the sauna. Her watch has stopped working and she doesn't want to be late for dinner, which they've ordered for seven. She says she tends to lose all count of time, and asked me if it wasn't too much trouble to check up she's out of here by six-forty. In fact, I'm a bit late because I got delayed chatting to David Lydgate.' I noted she looked a bit self-conscious as she mentioned his name.

'That's a bit beyond the call of duty, isn't it? Running after Iris Forbes.' Lissa shrugged prettily.

'The customer is always right, etcetera. And Iris is a millionaire's wife. They travel a lot. We want to be among the top places for service with a smile as well as facilities.

'Well, it looks as if she's still there. Or hasn't remembered to turn the light out.' A pencil-thin line of light showed under the door to the sauna-room. Lissa pushed it open and we went in. The place seemed unbearably hot. From the end cubicle a croaking sort of noise was coming. Lissa made towards it, a frown creasing her forehead. The sound was beginning to sound like someone with a very bad throat trying to call 'Help'.

'I can't open the door. Barry, come and help me.' She was tugging to no avail.

'Here, leave it to me.' Out loud I called, 'It's all right, Mrs Forbes. It's Lissa and Barry Vaughan. We'll have you out in a tick.' The door certainly seemed to be jammed, but a few hefty tugs and it shot open. A burning blast of air billowed out. I stood back modestly as Lissa stumbled in and emerged, half-supporting Iris Forbes, draped in a towel. Her attractively sun-tanned skin had turned to the colour of a ripe lobster and she was gleaming and dripping with sweat and gasping for breath.

'Barry, turn the thermostat down. It's there.' Lissa indicated. I did so, noting at the same time that it was up to a far higher temperature than it should have been. Silly woman, giving us a turn like that! Lissa was ministering to her, and looking anxious.

'I don't like the look of her at all, Barry. Once she's cooled down a bit in the shower I think we'd better get her into the air. She said something about her clothes. Can you see them? They weren't in the cubicle.' I couldn't Eventually, I found them haphazardly strewn over the floor in another cubicle. I handed them to Lissa, with some delicacy. Looking for a lady's scanties is not in the normal day's work at Woodfield Tech. And the whole thing was looking decidedly odd. Iris Forbes certainly hadn't seemed like the kind of absent-minded screwball who would take off her clothes in one cubicle and take a sauna in another. Or turn up the heat to danger-point.

Iris seemed to have recovered somewhat by the time

we'd walked her round in the cool evening breeze outside for a while. I couldn't help reflecting that it was a good thing she was such a health fiend. Glamorous lovely though she was, she was no chicken, and someone with a heart condition could very well have passed out in the conditions we had just left. She had now embarked on an angry diatribe to Lissa. I homed in on the end part.

'But, Iris, you're not suggesting that someone adjusted the heat to that level, wedged the door somehow so that you couldn't open it, and took your clothes from outside the cubicle!'

'That's exactly what I'm suggesting!' Sapphire eyes flashed. The bright red face was now partly the result of anger as well as excess heat. 'I dropped off to sleep for a bit over my book, and when I awoke it seemed far too hot, so I tried to get out of the cubicle. The door was jammed tight. I'd pulled it to, but not tightly. And I'd set the thermostat to a perfectly normal temperature. I shouted and shouted, but no one came. I felt like I was suffocating. I even soaked an end of the towel in the water left in the jug and put it over my face, to help me breathe. Then I remembered you had promised to come over and collect me. I'd no idea of the time – I seemed to have been in there hours, but of course in danger situations people always think that. However, I stopped trying the door, and concentrated on preserving my strength, so that when you did come, Lissa, I'd still be conscious. I don't think I would have been if you'd been five minutes later.'

'Are you absolutely sure you didn't undress in one cubicle and then decide to use another, and forget about it?'

'I assure you, my clothes were piled up on top of my sandals outside the cubicle you found me in. Now, I didn't turn up that heating myself, I didn't jam the door, and my

103

clothes didn't get up and walk. Which to my mind suggests a very nasty and unfunny practical joke by someone!'

As is usual, guests had ordered dinner for different times. However, by eight o'clock, everybody seemed to be gathered in the dining-room, the earliest diners on their final course and the newest arrivals scanning the menu. The Forbes had not put in an appearance. I had filled Dee in on the sauna-room incident, and we were speculating on who and why, in lowered voices, when Andrew Forbes strode into the dining-room. Just so might he have stormed the boardroom or marched in to confront a rival trying to muscle in on his territory. There was one of those round brass bells with a button on the top, sitting on a sideboard. Andrew banged on it. His eyes were glittering like the Ancient Mariner's, and, like that worthy, there was no doubt he had a tale to unfold. Gradually, table chatter died away. Beside us, Stephen raised an eyebrow at Maddy Lang. For once, the two of them appeared quite chummy, and the lovely Lissa was sitting with David Lydgate. She looked worried, as well she might. After all, she was Excelsior Holidays rep., a responsibility that was beginning to sit rather heavily on her slender shoulders.

'My wife,' began Andrew Forbes, without any pre-amble, 'has this evening been subjected to a harrowing and frightening ordeal.' He proceeded to describe what had happened, with considerable dramatic emphasis. He was, there was no doubt about it, an angry man.

'Naturally,' he concluded, 'I should be glad to know anything that sheds light on this matter. In my opinion this practical joker, for want of a better name, should be apprehended and punished. However, my wife, though she is too shaken and upset to even join me for dinner, says she is content to let the matter drop. I respect her wishes. But if anything of a similar nature happens in the course of our stay here, I shall be obliged to take certain measures.' He did not add 'I'm warning you,' but the message was loud and clear. I felt sorry for Lissa, who was looking pale and shaken.

Conversation was gradually resumed. Forbes strode out as histrionically as he strode in, probably to a supper tray in their room. Or perhaps he had decided to drive Iris to Stratford or Cheltenham to dine. Eric Coventry was looking oddly amused.

'A great sense of timing, Mrs Forbes,' he remarked, to no one in particular. It seemed an odd remark. Probably he meant Mr Forbes. Nora Hilton, whom he was sitting with, looked mildly enquiring, but he addressed himself to his *boeuf en daube*. At the next table, Karen Margolis, superb in an oyster-coloured silk sheath, shot him a look of virulent hatred. I was startled. They had been playing mixed doubles earlier with the Faircloughs, and had seemed amicable enough then. I wondered what Eric had done to tread on the fair Karen's toes.

'Maybe he's valued her jewels for her,' whispered Dee, giggling. She had either read my mind, or intercepted Karen's deadly glance, or both. On a holiday like this, perhaps one of the most interesting things was the shifting relationships. Some of which we would probably never know. Well, hadn't a book called *Grand Hotel* been written and filmed? Perhaps not every guest had a story behind them, but surely some of them did.

Ron Fairclough was telling Linda that she was to stay away from the sauna-room, and she was looking mutinous. David Lydgate had a hand resting on Lissa's, on the table. He was offering sympathy and advice. Or something. I shot a glance at Stephen Marriner, but he didn't appear to have noticed. Thank goodness. He was deep in a discussion of hubris in Shakespeare's tragedies and problem plays with Maddy Lang. She was supplying

surprisingly intelligent comments. Dee was listening in
avidly. As an Eng Lit. graduate, these learned analyses
attract her.

'Why don't you take your coffee over and join in?'

'Are you being sarcastic, Barry? I don't think I'd be
welcome, somehow.'

'Kate and Petruchio, huh?'

'Could be.'

It was as the Faircloughs started to rise that Lissa moved
into action. She banged on the bell Andrew Forbes had
used to such avail earlier, and again voices were stilled.

'Good evening, ladies and gentlemen. Now that you've
had a chance to sample some, or even all, of the activities
Avondale Country Club had to offer, we – that is,
Excelsior Holidays – thought you might like a little
diversion. So tomorrow night we propose a fancy-dress
party! There will be an orchestra laid on in the ballroom
– you may not all have located that yet. And some
professional entertainment. With, of course, plenty to
eat and drink! Now, if you are worrying about costumes,
don't! There is a firm in Cheltenham which has a wide
range to select from. Just apply to me for the details. And
for those of you who can't get into Cheltenham to order
your costumes tomorrow, a representative will visit the
hotel in the afternoon, with a good selection. So whether
you fancy going as a skinhead or as Little Bo Peep, there
should be something to suit you! I'm looking forward to
it, and I'm sure you'll thoroughly enjoy yourselves too.'

She sat down, to the accompaniment of clapping. Ron
Fairclough set up a cheer, which was taken up by Stephen
Marriner and David Lydgate, who then eyed each other
suspiciously.

'Good for you, Lissa', said Dee later, in the bar,
where we had repaired for Gaelic coffee. 'It sounds
very exciting – and took away the sting of earlier

106

happenings nicely!' David Lydgate, at Lissa's elbow, sniffed crossly.

'Poor Lissa. What she went through! Really, that Forbes woman seems to be a sacred cow, but if you ask me, she's a cow full stop!' Dee blinked. These seemed remarkably harsh words for the gentlemanly David Lydgate. We both looked at Lissa Stirling with a new respect. In her simple grey dress she seemed rather like an attractive air hostess. Or perhaps a more glamorous Jane Eyre. Not a *femme fatale*. But, first Stephen Marriner, and now David Lydgate? Of course, many people considered air hostesses as sex symbols. And Jane Eyre had managed to get proposals from two highly eligible men. Hadn't she?

'What,' Dee asked later, as we stretched out in bed, Bella snoring slightly at our feet, 'are we going to go as?'

'Haven't a clue. It really depends on what costumes are in stock, doesn't it?'

'Suppose so. Seems a pity to waste Bella – and leave her out, poor lamb. If they have any 1930s gear we could go as Nick and Nora. With Astra.'

'I suppose we could. I had rather thought of Napoleon and Josephine.'

'Napoleon and Josephine didn't have a dog, that we know of. Anyway you're too tall and not pudgy enough for Napoleon.'

'I could pad myself out.' Dee ignored this.

'Or Lord Nelson and Emma Hamilton', I offered.

'They didn't have a dog either.' I know when I'm beaten.

Chapter Eight

A BIT OF BLACKMAIL
BARRY

We decided to go into Cheltenham in the morning. As Dee pointed out, if we left the choosing of costumes to the representative's selection, not only would the choice be limited, but it would entail an undignified free-for-all scramble.

'Too dire, darling. Anyway, if we leave early, we'll get the pick of the bunch.' She had the same determined glint in her eye as I remember seeing every year as the time for the London sales – January or June – came round. A time when the adage about the female of the species being more deadly than the male is constantly borne out, and your Ms Average – if there is any such thing – becomes a ruthless Elizabeth I, a chariot-to-battle Boadicea.

'I thought you'd decided we were going as those wretched Nick and Nora types.' If I sounded pettish, it was because I was beginning to get just a tiny bit weary of the *alter egos* Dee had chosen for us at the time of the odd events at Wentworth Hall, a couple of years back.

'Well, perhaps you're getting a bit tired of poor Nick and Nora, Barry. Anyway,' she added, 'I might get a suitable evening dress, shoestring straps and all, but I'd have to have my hair cut and styled appropriately in those flat waves and I don't want to.'

'Ah, now we're getting to it. Dee, your motives are seldom pure and never simple.'

'Oscar Wilde said that – only it might have been the other way round, I'm not sure,' my nearest and dearest pointed out astringently.

'I know – he had all the best lines. Which is why they get pinched so often by people like me. Imitation being the best form of flattery.'

Anyway, we applied to Lissa for details, as instructed, and arrived nice and early at the costumiers, which proved to be situated in a private house in a quiet road, where racks upon racks of fascinating garments were kept hanging in deep, built-in cupboards, and wigs on wig-stands, fans, headgear of various kinds and paste tiaras and necklaces ornamented the tops of bureaux and tables. As you might guess, we spent some considerable time in this Aladdin's cave of treasure.

By this time we emerged, it was, I decided, time for brunch anyway, if not lunch, and Dee opted for the café-bar of the Everyman theatre. We sat on spindly black steel chairs at a marble-topped round table with a small Perrier bottle on it filled with pale-gold and pink carnations. Dee studied the menu and I studied the brick wall at the side, which had framed playbills and photos on it – not too interesting, except for a nice coloured picture of Adelina Patti, a good portrait in chalks of Noel Coward and a photo of Gertie Lawrence, her face looking surprisingly long and pointy-chinned.

'Scones with cream and apricot jam, toast and a pot of Earl Grey – how does that grab you?' Dee enquired. I had been hoping for something more sustaining, and said so.

'In that case, we'd have to go up to the restaurant on the second floor.' Dee indicated to her left, where a curving stairway with a brass rail led up to a wine bar on the first floor, and, beyond that, a lift in the lobby soared to higher regions.

'Anyway, it's not lunchtime yet, and there'll be something at the hotel.'

'Oh, all right.' Giving in to Dee on minor matters pays off, as she's more likely to defer to my judgement in major ones – sometimes.

While the waitress took the order, I observed the other people in the café. This was particularly easy to do, as there were wooden pillars at intervals along the brick wall to my right, down the length of the room, and a cabinet with a mirror was fixed sideways to the pillar nearest me, at such an angle that it was possible to see people at the other end of the room in it. There weren't many, and they were mainly young, one mother having a baby in a pushchair beside her table. A murmur of voices drifted towards me – a blend of soft regional and clipped 'educated' London. A couple of young men in jeans leaned against the bar, deep in discussion. And . . . there is always the unexpected in life.

The order arrived. Dee poured out the tea. I munched toast thoughtfully.

'As I was saying,' Dee repeated patiently, 'it's a good thing they deliver the costumes to the hotel for us. I'd like to have a look at a couple of shops, before we go back, and we won't have to worry about lugging them round.'

'We could always have left them in the car,' I pointed out vaguely.

'I suppose . . . Barry, what's the matter with you? You look as if you've seen something nasty in the woodshed.'

110

'No, but I've seen something intriguing in the mirror. Look at that cabinet, Dee, and tell me who you see at the very end of the room, at the table right against the wall.' Dee obeyed. She piled some cream and jam on a scone and bit into it.

'Delicious! Well, they do say necessity makes strange bedfellows, and I suppose fancy dress parties can throw up surprising combinations. I expect Stephen and Eric teamed up to select costumes. Maybe they're going to go together as a pair – I wonder what as?'

'Feasible – but look again at the expression on Stephen Marriner's face. I can't lip-read what he's saying, but whatever it is, it's angry.'

'Mmm – I see what you mean. Eric, on the other hand, looks urbane. How fascinating. Oh dear, Barry – Stephen's just pushed his chair back. He's striding out, leaving Eric with the bill. Do you think he'll see us? It's embarrassing.'

'Well – we can hardly dive under the table. He doesn't know we've seen him splitting in high dudgeon. Just concentrate on your scone and don't look at the mirror.'

Our table was at the window of the café, near the door leading to lobby and exit. Stephen paused fractionally in his long-legged stride as he saw us. His face was still stormy, but he made a conscious effort to smile as he nodded to us. He went out without speaking, however. Probably couldn't trust himself to, as Dee remarked a moment later.

As we drove back to the hotel, I told Dee about the little shop in Prestwick, nearby, where the Queen Mother stopped off and was greeted with a bunch of flowers every time.

'You're a cornucopia of quaint facts and anecdotes – do you know that, Barry?' She was temporarily diverted, then returned to what was on her mind.

'There's odd things going on at that hotel. People's relationships, for a start.'

'Like?'

'Well, the Lissa-Stephen-Maddy-David situation. Add to that Geoff and Ellen, and is David interested in Ellen as well as Lissa? Then, what's with Eric Coventry and Stephen Marriner?'

'And,' I recalled, 'I saw Karen looking at Eric as if she loathed him last night. He's definitely done or said something to both her and Stephen. If looks could kill!'

'And there was the riding-school incident. If it wasn't a schoolkid's prank . . . then it was something rather sinister and frightening. Not to mention what happened to Iris. There doesn't seem to be any connection between the two, yet I've got this weird feeling that there is somehow.'

'Well, stop thinking about it. We're here to enjoy ourselves – remember? The fancy-dress do tonight should be fun . . . you make a very fetching Emma Hamilton.'

We had ended up as Nelson and Lady Hamilton after all – Dee said I was too tall and not corpulent enough for Napoleon, and she wouldn't wear anything Elizabethan, because the weather was too warm, and we couldn't think of many historical couples on the spur of the moment at the costumiers.

Lunch was a buffet affair, again, with people drifting in and out. There were sly looks and bursts of laughter, as we tried to find out from each other what we were going as. No one telling – with the exception of ingenuous Geoff Routledge, who announced he was a spaceman; because, as he explained 'I just couldn't think of anything else.' Little Nora Hilton was looking excited, two pink spots on her cheeks, and her eyes bright.

'I haven't had so much fun since I was a girl!' she exclaimed, adding rather wistfully, 'There were lots of parties then, including fancy-dress. I can remember

112

dancing till dawn, and getting tiddly on champagne – of course the Charleston was all the rage then, my dears, but I was never very good at it, I'm afraid.'

'It's odd to think of you as a flapper, Nora,' Karen said, smiling.

'I suppose it must be, looking at me now, dear,' Nora replied placidly. 'But they were very gay times – in the old-fashioned sense of the word. The trouble with you young folk is that you can never imagine that we were once like you. Well – perhaps not quite the same. People were ambitious then, but without the drive and slog there seems to be today, especially among the girls. Though a streamlined sports car that went fast was the great desire of all the young men – some things don't change, it seems!'

'Quite right, Nora,' Andrew Forbes agreed heartily. 'I remember when I got my first car – not a sports model, I'm afraid; I was far too poor for that. But it was a status symbol all the same – without "wheels" you were nothing. And I tinkered around with that old souped-up banger with all the loving care of a young mother bathing her infant! I remember once . . . ' And off he launched into reminiscences, his angry mood of the previous evening seemingly a thing of the past. Iris caught Dee's eye and made a humorous grimace.

'Someone stop him, or he'll go on for hours,' she murmured, the fondness in her gaze as she looked at her husband belying the tartness in her voice.

'And what are you going as, Iris?' Dee enquired innocently.

'That would be telling!' Iris laughed, and then relented.

'Poor Dee – you're not having very much luck in finding out our costumes, are you? I'm afraid your approach isn't subtle enough! Never mind – you can come along to our room and see mine, if you like. I'm afraid you'll be disappointed – I'm like Geoff. I picked something very uninspired. I'd welcome your opinion, though.'

Dee took up the offer with alacrity, polishing off her strawberry mousse in record time and vanishing in Iris's wake like Atalanta pursuing the apple, while Andrew regaled us with more reminiscences.

'Go on, Nora, do tell us what you're going as,' I wheedled.

'Well – I could give you a few surprises, I think,' she twinkled, in her best Miss Marple manner. 'Shall I just say – that a crystal ball is involved.'

'A fortune-teller!' Karen exclaimed. 'Marvellous! Do you really tell fortunes for real, Nora?'

'Well – yes. As a matter of fact, I do. At least, I used to, to amuse my daughters and their friends when they were younger. Of course, I made a lot of it up. But, the astonishing thing is that I found out I really am psychic, apparently. I found myself "seeing" things that turned out to be true, and when I got interested in palmistry I got even better. I gave it up eventually, because it started to frighten me – having these "special powers".'

There was a short, respectful silence. Then Lissa, who had come up to join our group, interjected excitedly, 'But you must, Nora! Just think. It'll be the star turn of the evening! People won't want to dance all the time, and once the fancy-dress parade is over, things might get a bit flat. Do, do, dear Nora,' she pleaded coaxingly. 'It'll give us all something more to look forward to. Won't it?' And she turned to me.

'Certainly,' I agreed gallantly. 'Nora, you'll be the star of the show!'

'Well . . . ' Reluctance warred with gratification in her sweet little face.

'Be a sport, Mrs Hilton.' Geoffrey Routledge added his plea. 'I've never had my fortune told,' he added, in the manner of a child asking for a ride on the big dipper. Nora capitulated.

'Very well – if you all want me to . . . '

'We do!' we chorused in unison.

'Then I suppose I shall have to bow gracefully to the inevitable. But be warned, I must say what I see, and it might not all be to your liking.'

There didn't seem to be much activity that afternoon. The guests had either dispersed to their rooms to try on their costumes, or were filing in to a late lunch. As I left the buffet table, Ellen floated in, a dreamy smile wreathing her face. She made straight for Geoff.

'Geoff, darling, it's going to be a fabulous evening. You'll adore my costume – it's fantastic. "Queen of the Night" – sort of black and dark purple, with gold stars and moons all over it – well, the moons are silver – I look absolutely Go-orgeous!'

'You always do, Ellen.'

There was something appealingly childlike about both of them – the admiring swain and the naively narcissistic idol, coming to life with an audience before whom she knows she looks her best. This holiday was producing one idyll, anyway – I hoped it wouldn't be shattered too rudely by reality when the time came to go home. Lissa, charmingly businesslike as ever, homed in.

'Ellen, darling, I know you're on holiday, and goodness knows I don't want to spoil it for you, but, well, you are a public figure, you know, and I was hoping that you'd give us a few songs this evening. There's the orchestra, and I can arrange for you to have a truly magnificent guitar, because I know you haven't got your own with you. And,' she added, 'it won't be just us, because we've got lots of the club members coming in, till eleven o'clock only, of course, because the hotel is out of bounds to non-residents after that. You will, won't you, Ellen – I'm absolutely *counting* on you!'

'Lissa Stirling, you're really good,' I thought. I could understand how she held down her undeniably demanding post. First Nora, now Ellen. She would have made a good theatrical agent – or confidence trickster, if she wasn't so basically wholesome. I could tell from Karen Margolis's expression that she shared my opinion. I didn't wait to hear Ellen's answer – I knew what it would be. The true performer – which Ellen, in spite of her aura of childishness, at times, indisputably was, – cannot resist the chance to appear, and hear the applause, holiday or no holiday.

Checking that Dee was not in our room – either she was still exchanging woman-talk with Iris Forbes, or she had moved on to pastures new – I decided to take a stroll round the grounds. I bumped into Stephen Marriner – literally – coming round a corner of the building. He was walking slowly, head down, hands in the pockets of his jeans, an abstracted frown on his face.

'Hey, watch where you're going,' I said lightly.

'Sorry.' He glared at me for an instant, not looking the least bit sorry about anything. Then he said, abruptly, 'Want a drink? I could do with one.' I glanced back towards the café at the front of the house, festooned with fairy lights which were not turned on yet.

'I don't think they're serving alcohol yet.'

'That doesn't matter. I have some whisky in my room. Anyway, it's more private there.' I followed him. If he wanted to disburden his soul, I was willing to be an attentive listener.

When we were settled with glasses filled with miniatures

116

of Glenfiddich, garnished with ice cubes, Stephen began. Without preamble.

'I expect you and your wife are wondering why I was with Eric Coventry in the Everyman café.'

'It didn't seem to be from choice.'

'Damned right it wasn't. That poisonous little turd is blackmailing me.'

'Oh.' I wasn't entirely surprised.

'Yes – it appears he is about to "retire", in every sense of the word, and he assured me this was a one-off. Quite eloquently. I almost believed him. But you never know with blackmailers, do you?'

'So I'm given to understand. I've never actually had that nasty experience, though.'

'No, I suppose you wouldn't. Count yourself lucky.' He drained his glass and went for a refill.

'How much?' I asked.

'Ten grand, but he'll settle for seven.' I whistled.

'A sizeable sum.'

'And a damnably clever move. I'm no pauper, with this *Baron* series, but on the other hand I've got heavy mortgage commitments. It's just about the amount I could afford. I suppose,' he added truculently, 'you want to know what for.'

'Well, I did guess from an earlier conversation that there might be something.'

'There often is, with our profession,' Stephen said bitterly. 'Shoddy deals, money owed, gambling debts, gay episodes, illegitimate kids – the lot.'

'So what is it in your case?' I asked quietly. He obviously wanted to tell someone, and he'd picked me as confidant. Stephen shrugged, and began to pace round the room restlessly.

'Not as bad as some. Hell, I knew of one guy who got into such a mess that he staged a mock suicide by drowning and disappeared to live in the wilds of rural France. Of course, someone he knew decided to take a "get away from it all" holiday and bumped into him supping with the locals in a quaint little caff, so all was out. I'd never do that.'

'But your career would be affected adversely?'

'Too right it would.' Stephen laughed savagely. 'Male strip star for a couple of months (under a pseudonym, of course) might just about get by – but actor in porno movies doesn't quite fit in with the image of *The Baron* – not to mention all those Shakespearian heroes! From Soho to Stratford! It makes a good title, don't you think?'

'How blue were the movies?'

'To be honest, I don't know. I just did my bits, so to speak, grabbed the gelt, and got out. Puerile plots, and a lot of heaving and groaning on top of some poor busty cow who couldn't pay the rent any more than I could. One of them was called *Nights in the Harem* and another was *The Sex Slaves*. I never saw the finished products. But you get the picture.'

Yes, I got the picture. I forbore to ask him what his pseudonym was. Enough is enough. Dee wouldn't have had such inhibitions.

'And he threatened to leak it to the gutter press, I suppose?'

'The gutter press and any other press that's interested. So bang goes my contract – and my career.' I nodded. No good telling Stephen he'd get over it. He wouldn't. Eric Coventry had him by the short and curlies, and he knew it.

'How did he find out?'

'Sleazy contacts in Soho. A great pity, because the company that made the blue movies is now disbanding, and they're going to be on the scrap heap. They weren't

118

very good blue movies, you understand. Another month, and they'll be up in smoke. Except for *Sins of Don Juan*. I was Don Juan in that one. The prints are still available, and Eric can get hold of them.'

'Have another drink,' I urged sympathetically. It was a case where alcohol seemed called for.

Stephen sank down onto his bed, looking suddenly weary and defeated.

'I suppose you despise me, don't you?'

'Not at all. I can see the situation vividly. Young, ambitious, no money, desperate for food and rent, and other people in the profession did it, so why not you?'

'Exactly. But you wouldn't have, would you?'

'I don't exactly have the physique for *Sins of Don Juan*. Whose exploits, I feel, have been magnified and exploited for literary purposes for centuries, anyway.' For the first time, Stephen seemed amused.

'I like you, Barry. And I like your wife. And your humour. I've read one of your books, by the way. Good stuff.'

'Oh, really? Which one?' I was pleased.

'*Framed Murder*.'

'My last. I like it, but most people think *Penny for the Guy* and *Proof of the Pudding* are better.

'I'll buy them,' Stephen promised. 'And publicise them. If I ever get out of this mess.'

I returned to the matter in hand.

'I can see,' I volunteered carefully, 'that the great British public might not be impressed. Or,' – I paused – 'a nice girl like Lissa Stirling, for example.'

'Are you kidding? Dear Lissa would be horrified. She'd say, "After all, Stephen, one has standards," using the royal "one". Or words to that effect.'

'And Madeleine Lang?'

'Ah, Maddy. Now, that's a different kettle of fish. She'd tease me unmercifully, but I think she'd understand. Might even be supportive, in her odd way. Maddy and I are two of a kind. If she hadn't been born with the proverbial silver spoon in her mouth, she'd no doubt have been appearing in something like *Nights in the Harem* herself.' He kicked moodily at the carpet.

'Still, I was fool, there's no getting away from it. I should have driven a lorry, learned to lay bricks, anything.'

'No good crying over spilt milk,' I commented crisply. 'The burning question is – what are you going to do?'

'Bump off Eric, perhaps.' Momentarily, he looked savage.

'Which is what I'd like to do, believe me.'

'Inadvisable. What about the police?' Stephen shook his head emphatically.

'No, no, and again no. Eric would deny it, and probably go ahead with the publicity, out of spite. Through someone else. No, I'll have to pay up. Before the end of the holiday, or shortly after, depending on when I can get the cash.'

'It's to be a cash payment, then?'

'Oh yes. Untraceable, in case I decide to shout afterwards. In return, I get the print of *Don Juan*.'

'I hate to think of him getting away with it.'

'So do I, Barry, believe me. But that creature has his comeuppance coming to him one of these days, from someone. You can bet your bottom dollar on that. Anyway, thanks for listening to the saga.'

'Don't mention it.' I nearly added, 'Any time,' but decided it would be a remark in poor taste. I left him, looking gloomy again, and feeling a considerable distaste for Mr Eric Coventry. It crossed my mind that this might not be the only little blackmail racket he had going. Everyone needs cash for their retirement – but there is a limit.

Chapter Nine

A REAL MURDER
DEE

The Forbes' room was very nice – as usual there was the historical motif, with a china plaque proclaiming 'Charles II' on the door and a portrait of that rakish monarch on the wall.

'Can I offer you anything?' Iris moved towards the small fridge which all the rooms contained.

'A Perrier water would be nice.' I'd already had some wine at lunch and wanted to keep a clear head for the evening. Iris poured me a glass and another for herself.

'Dee, you *must* try some of my special liqueur as well. Just a *soupçon*,' she wheedled, with a persuasive smile.

'Oh – all right. Just a very tiny drop, mind.'

Iris produced a plain unlabelled bottle of pale amber liquid, and poured what seemed to me a considerable amount than the 'tiny drop' I'd requested, into a second glass, and another for herself. I held it up and regarded it with interest.

'Cheers.' I took a sip, and then another. The liquid slid down my throat like silk, and a comfortable warmth suffused me. I began to feel relaxed. And benevolent. And even euphoric. It is perfectly true, these are effects produced by many liqueurs, but what I was not prepared for was the aftertaste – a truly paradisiacal flavour compounded of honey and almonds and herbs and fruits. I gasped, and Iris, sipping her own glass, smiled. No doubt she had often seen this reaction – that is, if she was in the habit of handing out dollops of this glorious ambrosia for free.

'Iris, this stuff is glorious. Words fail me!'

'I thought you'd like it.'

'"Like" is the understatement of the year. I'm crazy about it. Where do you get it?'

'I don't. It's specially distilled by monks in Turkey.'

'I thought most people in Turkey were Muslim.'

'These monks are Christian – they settled there a couple of centuries ago – at least, their predecessors did.'

'I've got a friend who's got a villa in Turkey. In the south.'

'I'm afraid she's nowhere near the source. This monastery is perched up near the top of a craggy mountain in an area inland from the Black Sea. It's spectacular country, but frightening to drive through, with great drops and ravines everywhere. We couldn't take a car up to the monastery, so had to get up there on foot – and when we discovered the liqueur Andrew promptly bought all their remaining stock – we had it taken down to the car by mules.'

'How fascinating. Has it a name.'

'Not really. But Andrew and I call it "1001 nights" because it's as intriguing as one of Scheherazade's stories. We always carry a couple of bottles round with us. I suppose when the supply runs out we'll have to go back to Turkey again and pick up another lot.'

'Nice to have the chance.' I commented enviously. Iris shrugged gracefully.

'Oh, it certainly is. I'm not denying that for a moment.

I guess we seem pretty rich and spoiled to you, Dee. But we've both worked terribly hard in the past, especially Andrew. And believe me, we've had our ups and downs in life.' For a moment a new disturbing expression flitted across her face – a pinched, hungry, angry look. I murmured something soothing, and Iris jumped up.

'I was going to show you my costume. I'm not sure about it. I think now maybe it's a bit drab, and I should change it – what do you think?' She drew a cellophaned gown on a hanger out of the wardrobe and unveiled it. It was a satin 1930s style evening dress, with a cowl neck and a pattern of beads encrusting the bodice, but lightly, in curves like fronds of fern. The colour was a muted silver-grey, and there were grey buckled high-heeled shoes and a cloak in an almost gun-metal shade to go over the gown.

'I thought I'd set my hair with bobby-pins, in those waves – Marcel waves or whatever they were called. I know how to do it. And wear a long string of pearls and pearl earings. And call myself just "1930s woman".' I laughed. Iris looked a bit hurt.

'Sorry, Iris – you see, it's just that Barry and I were going to go in a similar style, but we opted for Nelson and Lady Hamilton instead. Your costume does look understated, it's true, but I should think it'll look fabulous on. Why not try it on now and show me?'

While Iris retired to the bathroom, I amused myself by examining the cosmetics and photos on the dressing-table top. There was one of Andrew, smiling triumphantly with a huge trout he'd just landed, a family group of Andrew and Iris, both a few years younger, outside a handsome looking mansion, Canadian-style, with two wholesome-looking young men, and a much older photo, a bit faded, of a lovely, laughing young woman in a tennis dress, brandishing her racquet aloft. Her hair was tumbled in curls around her shoulders, and when I looked closer, I could see that the features were Iris's. She looked to be about the same age as one of her stepsons in the other photo. Well, Iris was still beautiful but she wasn't a young girl any more. Still, I should be so lucky, if I were to look like Iris in my fifties. I don't have those glorious sapphire eyes, of course, and I doubt if my complexion will ever be as clear. Perhaps I should eschew alcohol now, and stick to mineral waters completely. On the other hand, some sacrifices are too great to make, and I've known some very passable second-class complexions.

At that moment, Iris emerged from the bathroom. Even without the hair set in the appropriate style, she looked lovely, and I told her so.

'You're beautifully understated, Iris – you'll make the rest of us seem tawdry in comparison. Anyway, it's far too late to change your costume now – you're stuck with it. I'm afraid!' Iris didn't look too displeased with the notion.

'Poor Andrew. He's going as a cowboy, Stetson and all. It suits his style, but we're not going to be a very good mix n'match, I'm afraid!'

'Never mind,' I said vaguely. I wandered over to the dressing-table and picked up the tennis photo again.

'You look awfully pretty in this, Iris.' There was a little gasp and I looked up just in time to catch a grimace – a twist of the features. 'Just as pretty as you do now, in fact,' I added quickly with a laugh, to cover up my gaffe, if there was one. Funny – I hadn't put Iris Forbes down as one of the world's vain women – I'd thought her far too sensible for that. Still – who knows how any of us are likely to react in our fifties, confronted with the girl we once used to be? Only in that case, why keep the reminder on the dressing-table? A homage to mortality, like Sarah Bernhardt going to sleep in a coffin at night –

or just plain nostalgia? What did it matter, either way? It was time I was tracking down my errant husband.

'And obviously just as keen on tennis – I'd challenge you to a singles game, but I know you'd wipe me off the court.' I drained the last few delicious drops of '1001 Nights' and sidled towards the door.

'Thanks for the gorgeous liqueur, Iris. The costume's fine – really it is. We'll see you and Andrew tonight – maybe Andrew will give me a dance. I've always wanted to dance with a handsome cowboy!'

Iris laughed warmly, and whatever odd undercurrents there had been in the preceding minutes seemed to have disappeared, as she opened the door for me.

'Thanks for your opinion about the dress, Dee. You're right, of course. See you this evening.'

When I got back to our room Barry was there. He looked thoughtful. We decided to go for a walk to clear our heads (particularly mine, after my draught of '1001 Nights'). We took Bella with us and went up the main road and down a side road with a village store and a postbox. Eric Coventry was just placing a small package into its mouth. He paused fractionally as we turned the corner and came into view, then pushed the package in and nodded at us. I nodded back. Barry ignored him pointedly. He's not usually so rude.

'Methinks he did start, like a guilty thing surpriz'd,' I murmured to Barry. My loved one snorted sarcasticallly.

'That one wouldn't know what guilty feelings were if you served them up on a plate to him.'

'My, my, my – do you know something I don't?'

We were ambling past attractive brick houses, not old, but well-designed. Some had white porticoes, some had latticed windows. All had smooth, lush green lawns and well-tended flower-beds. Bees bumbled, and the fragrance of honeysuckle vied with that of roses. It all bespoke money, and the kind of peace which money can buy when the hard day is done. The sleazy Soho story Barry told me couldn't have been more at variance with this Eden. And yet, I suppose, there might well have been an Eric Coventry or two tucked away behind the façade – probably innocuous-seeming men whose only vices appeared to be an over-indulgence in golf or the occasional £50 on a horse at Cheltenham. I felt upset by the story, probably because I liked Stephen, and somehow I saw him now in a different light. Mud sticks. Still, I felt for him. *Sins of Don Juan* might have its comic side, but for Stephen it was anything but comic.

'And I'm pretty sure he's trying the same game with Karen Margolis,' Barry went on.

'Any proof – or just instinct?'

'Apart from the fact she's been giving him murderous looks, I went out for a think and saunter after hearing Stephen's tale – to try and think up some way of helping him, I suppose. Well, I didn't think of anything, but as I came by the swimming-pool I heard voices raised, or rather, *a* voice, and looked under the archway. Eric and Karen were standing near the pool – I got the impression it was a pre-arranged meeting because the area was deserted except for me – everyone trying on their costumes and so on.'

'What was she saying?' Barry tends to go in for novelistic preambles. Me, I like to get to the nitty-gritty a.s.a.p.

'I don't know what she *had* been saying, or him either.' Barry looked distinctly regretful.

'All I caught was "You can do your damnedest, you crooked conniving bastard!" She was yelling that. Then she lashed out and slapped his face. Rather him than me. Athletic girl, Karen. Packs quite a punch. She nearly toppled him right into the pool. At that point she started running for the archway – end of scene – and as I thought it might be embarrassing for her to bump straight into me – '

'Not to mention embarrassing for you.'

'Exactly – well, so I nipped down the side path towards the annexe bedrooms. I don't think she saw me. I hung around a bit till I thought they'd both have gone, then came back to our bedroom. Where you found me, shortly afterwards.'

'It's quite a hotbed of intrigue here, isn't it, Barry?'

'Well – I've known worse. But on the other hand, I admit, the place seems to be alive with incident and humming with undercurrents.'

'You've got a nice turn of phrase, on occasion, my love.'

'As the actress said to the bishop. But seriously, Dee, let's try and forget all about incidents and undercurrents this evening and enjoy the do. Speaking of which, when we reach that pretty thatched white cottage near the signpost, I vote we make tracks back to the hotel and have a nap before getting ready.'

'A nap, huh?'

'Yes. Just a nap,' Barry said firmly. 'I'm finding all these confidences and near-close encounters rather tiring.'

'Not to mention nipping down side paths.'

'Precisely. It's not so much the quick sprint, it's more the nervous strain.'

As it happened, I fell asleep, too. I woke to the sound of Barry doing his 'Shows of Rogers and Hammerstein' bit in the shower.

Half an hour later, as Barry was straightening his white stockings and adjusting his eyepatch, and I was concealing my cleavage with my Emma Hamilton fichu, a knock came on the door. It was little Linda Fairclough, with her husband sheepishly in attendance behind her. They had large sandwich-board playing cards back and front, and head-dresses. King and Queen of Diamonds. I guessed that Linda might have liked something more stylish and original, but that she wanted to go as a pair with Ron, and he had opted for the trite.

'You both look very striking,' I commented with perfect truth. They did. Original, no. Striking, yes. Black on white, and black robes beneath the playing cards.

'Thanks. You look terrific, too. I can see Barry is Lord Nelson, but who are you, Dee?'

'His mistress. Emma Hamilton.'

'Oh.'

'She was a barmaid who married a Lord and then Nelson met her,' Barry enlarged. 'After his death he left her as a bequest to the nation.'

'Oh. I don't think I'd like to be left to the nation,' Linda said thoughtfully.

'I daresay Emma wasn't too crazy about it either,' I put in.

'Have you seen the ballroom?' Linda was pink with excitement. This was obviously of much more moment than Emma Hamilton's feelings. 'It's gorgeous. It's that big room overlooking the terrace at the back of the house. There's a rostrum covered in royal blue and gold, and loads of flowers banked up around it, and the orchestra is tuning up. Mrs Hilton is all done up as a gypsy and she's got a booth in one corner. There are loads of outside people, club people, and some of them are in fancy dress as well. The rest are in evening gear. It's really swinging already.'

'Sounds OK. Where's the food, Ron?' Barry winked with his un-patched eye, and Ron grinned.

'Loads of nosh in the dining-room. And best bitter, too.'

'Let's go and inspect the bitter and leave the girls to inspect the guests.'

'Bet we have more fun,' I said.

'Bet you don't.' They vanished in one direction by the stairway and Linda and I took the other. There was a queue already forming outside Nora Hilton's booth. It was in royal blue with swages of silver material, in contrast to the blue and gold of the rostrum. The orchestra were playing some Jerome Kern, very Palm Court-ish, but no one was dancing yet, just mingling. Several clutched glasses, and there was a babble of voices. Ellen Starr was the cynosure of many eyes, and she looked just as gorgeous in her Queen of the Night costume as she had artlessly said she would. A slim and dashing David Lydgate, in Lincoln green, was talking to her. The hapless Geoff Routledge had been trapped in conversation by a dowager type in a Liberty evening dress. I nudged Linda.

'I bet inside that goldfish bowl helmet his eyes are swivelled right round to Ellen.' She giggled.

'Hasn't David Lydgate got nice legs?'

'*Very* nice legs.' We both admired them in silence for a moment.

'Oh look – there's Lissa. She's in Lincoln green too!' And very fetching she looked, with a green jerkin and hose and boots; her shining hair falling sleekly to her shoulders under a dashing little green hat with a jaunty feather. Her legs were nice, too. In fact, nice is an understatement. They went on for ever and were the kind that Betty Grable in her heyday would have insured for a million dollars.

'She must be Maid Marian. Strictly speaking,' I added, 'I don't think Maid Marian should be wearing Lincoln Green. More homespun grey.'

'Oh, Dee, does it matter? Lissa wouldn't look half as good in homespun grey.'

'You can say that again, kid.' The fact that she and David were going as a pair surely said something for the progress of their romance.

'Can you see anyone else we know?'

'Karen – she looks nice, too. I don't know the boy she's with.' I did. Norm, not in fancy dress, just a dinner suit, looking as if he felt he should have slipped into something more comfortable. Karen was Diana the Huntress, in a brief simple white tunic, with bow and quiver. Her splendid limbs were much in evidence. I would not have liked to have been the unfortunate deer that got in her way. She looked as if she could wield a mean bow and arrow.

Across the room, a laurelled Julius Caesar made conversation with a white rabbit. Eric Coventry! And he *did* make a good Caesar. I automatically swept the room with my eyes, looking for Stephen Marriner, but he was nowhere in evidence. Neither was Maddy Lang. Barry appeared at the door, beckoning us.

'You ain't seen nothing yet, kids. Go back to the staircase.' We did. An insouciant river boat gambler type in elegant dove-grey, frilled white shirt and a hat at a rakish angle was descending, on his arm a vision in a pale pink crinoline skirted frilled dress, tiny-waisted, her abundant dark tresses caught in a pink snood, and with a corsage of pink-and-white frilly blossoms. Stephen and Maddy, as Rhett Butler and the young Scarlett O'Hara.

I could hear 'ooh's' and 'ah's' and 'Aren't they fabulous?' and 'How did she get her waist squeezed in so tight?' and 'That's the best I've seen yet.' I was inclined to agree. Linda was quite overcome with admiration, and so was Ron, who had reappeared to claim her, cheerful in visage and lager-ish in breath.

'That's some dramatic entrance!'

'Well, they are both actors,' I pointed out. We made

131

our way back to the ballroom, in time to hear the orchestra strike up a waltz, as a burst of clapping greeted Stephen's and Maddy's entrance. Round and round they circled gracefully, moving in perfect accord, making the waltz somehow both an aesthetic and sensual experience. Gradually one couple joined, then another, then David Lydgate led Ellen Starr out onto the floor, and they were joined by Norm and Karen, looking rather incongruous in their ill-matched gear, and finally the dancing became general, with spectators perched on chairs at the edges, and a space left clear beyond the entry door to the ballroom, which was where Nora Hilton, alias Madame Zara, had her fortune-telling booth.

I wandered down to the orchestra end of the room, in search of Barry, but by the time I reached where he had last been standing, he had whisked Lissa Stirling off for a dance. I could see Iris Forbes, looking soignée and elegant in her 1930s get-up, dancing with the spaceman. From the tight expression on her face I guessed she was finding it a somewhat painful experience, to the feet, anyway.

Open doors at the side gave a tantalising glimpse of a balcony graced with a riot of flowers in stone urns, and a flight of greystone steps leading onto a sloping lawn. Beyond this there were flower-beds, a clump of trees, and, far to the right, the driveway curving around from the front of the building, past us at the back, and on towards the entrance gates. A couple of people had already drifted onto the balcony, and I suddenly spotted a somehow familiar figure that I yet could not immediately place, squeezing sideways through the doors back into the ballroom. He was dressed in formal dinner wear, but still managed to look out of place. Nevertheless, I saw him greeted by a woman I recognised as a Country Club member, a tennis-playing plain Jane who had beaten Eric Coventry in a singles game. Of course! This was the man

Barry and I had noticed with Eric in Great Malvern. I searched around for Barry and Lissa, but this time it was a dance later and Barry was giving Linda Fairclough a whirl. Lissa was temporarily on her own, the faint frown of responsibility creasing her forehead as she surveyed the ballroom. I hated to deepen that frown, but I approached nevertheless.

'Lissa, a word or two, if you don't mind.' I led her off further into the fringes of the dance floor, into a windowed recess.'

'I think,' I informed her, 'we might have a persona here who is not grata.' Lissa looked puzzled, as I suppose well she might.

'Would you mind making yourself a bit clearer, Dee?' I expanded. And expounded. Lissa pointed out that it was a rule Club members were allowed to invite a guest each to evening do's at the hotel. Naturally, since Club members were vetted strictly before being allowed to join, it was assumed that any guest they might choose to bring along with them would also be a bona fide good citizen.

'Anyway, Dee, one can hardly throw a guest out on the premise that he looks sneaky and you saw him in what you thought were suspicious circumstances with one of our party in Great Malvern. I mean, they both probably had a perfectly legitimate reason for being there, like you and Barry.' I sighed.

'Of course, Lissa, you're right. But do try and find out his name at any rate, and any info. And if I were you, I'd detail someone to keep a watch on any handbags that are left lying about.'

'All right.' She didn't look very happy, but she nodded. Her eye caught David Lydgate's across the room, and she visibly relaxed, and lifted her hand in a little wave. I guessed he'd soon claim her for a dance.

'You like David, don't you, Lissa?'

'Very much. Don't you?' But that wasn't what I'd meant, and we both knew it.

There was only a queue of two waiting at Madame Zara's booth, so I wafted up to join it, deciding that after this is was time for refreshments in the dining-room. On my way up the room to it I brushed by Iris. She was looking thoughtful and far-away. Andrew was somewhere in evidence, talking to a Club member (or guest).

'Coming to have your fortune told, Iris?'

'No. I don't believe in that sort of thing. Meddling with the unknown.' She sounded brusque and dismissive, and I was surprised.

'Oh. I see.' She had already turned away.

'Funny she's so against it,' a voice at my elbow remarked, 'I saw Nora, and she's simply marvellous!' It was Geoffrey, his spaceman's helmet thrown back to give him air. 'Karen says she's marvellous, too – though I got mainly nice things and I think Karen got some bad predictions – or home truths she didn't like. Can I interest you in a dance, Dee?'

'Er – no, Geoff. I'm next in line for Madame Zara, and I don't want to lose my place.' Well, it was true.

'Why don't you seek Ellen out,' I suggested. 'I haven't seen you dancing with her all evening so far, and you don't have all that much more time, because we're going to have some kind of entertainment, aren't we, including Ellen singing.'

'Well, the fact of the matter is, Dee, I'm not a very good dancer.' He looked uncomfortable and wretched.

'You mean Ellen's dainty toes are too good to be trodden on, but mine aren't?' I laughed. 'Well, I can see you don't want to do anything to put her off you, but why don't you get her a nice cool drink and take her out on the terrace, before it gets too crowded with stargazers?'

'Terrific idea. Bless you, Dee.'

'Any time. Just call me little old Cupid.'

I emerged from Madame Zara's booth, feeling decidedly thoughtful. Nora, in her gypsy costume, had presented a slightly play-acting figure to the eye at first, but she had been extremely matter-of-fact and apparently completely sincere about what she 'saw' for me. Granted, some of it was obvious things, but there were other things I don't see how she could possibly have known in advance, unless Barry had told her. Also, I was quite pleased to hear I would be going abroad at Christmas, and a lot of snowy scenery predicted (a ski-ing week was something Barry and I had almost decided on already) but I was startled to hear that we could expect an addition to our family within the next year and a half. Maybe this time Barry's and my efforts in the population increase stakes would come to something. Which was a hopeful and exciting thought. On the other hand, it might refer to a little friend for Bella. One never knows. Perhaps Iris is right about not mucking around with the unknown.

The final revelation, which I did not like one little bit, was that I was to come very near to sudden death in the very near future. Again, that was ambiguous. Did it mean I was going to be on the scene of someone else's death – or did it mean that I myself would be in danger of death? Either way, it was not an attractive prospect, and I found myself shivering as I emerged from the booth, leaving Nora looking reposeful and somehow trance-like.

'You're cold, Dee. Come and have a dance – it'll warm you up. Then I'll get you a wrap, if you like.'

'Make it a couple of dances – I've been feeling quite neglected!'

'Alas, Lady Hamilton, England expects every man to do his duty.'

135

'Especially when it involves young and lovely females, yes, I know. And I'm not quite sure about the historical accuracy of that remark, anyway!'

'Bother history, for once. You look deliciously pretty, Dee.'

'Thank you, kind sir – er, was that your good eye or your bad one speaking?' We joked our way round the floor, earning a few smiles and a few admiring looks. Obviously our costumes were a hit. Afterwards Barry escorted me to the dining-room, where I filled up a plate of delicious scraps for Bella and dispatched Barry with it, and to get my warm shawl. I ate hungrily; if I'd left it much longer nothing would have been left. The sound of cheering and clapping from the ballroom announced that the 'entertainment' was due to start. I licked some stray crumbs from my fingers, wiped them with a hanky, and trotted back, keeping a chair empty beside me for Barry. He joined me a few minutes later, in the middle of a comedian's patter which was moderately funny. There was a conjurer who did card tricks with members of the audience, a girl trio who sang very loudly, another comedian, and then the M.C. announced Ellen. She was already sitting waiting in position on the rostrum, with the orchestra, and as she stood up to bow, in her Queen of the Night costume, there was a storm of clapping. Ellen waited till it died down, bowed again, with smiling dignity, seated herself, and took her guitar. She sang beautifully, old favourites as well as a couple of new ones, and encores were demanded. At last she took her final bow and smilingly disappeared, and the orchestra packed up their instruments, as chairs scraped and a large section of the audience moved towards the door. It was nearly eleven, and time for Club members to get themselves off the premises, according to hotel rules.

Barry was chatting so I decided to fetch Bella and take

her for an evening walk. She was pleased to be let out and frisked along at my side. As we approached the swimming-pool area I could see the light shining under the archway, and wandered in. Immediately, I felt a spooky sense of unease, which Bella seemed to share, as she growled, then whined. The sky was very dark, with a few jewelled stars, and the water was dark, too – but in the shallow end, just near the steps, a figure floated face-down. It was wearing a white toga and a crown of laurel leaves hung half-way off its dark head.

I ran to the pool and panting and heaving, managed to get the sodden body out. The lower part of my flimsy dress was soaked, as far as my thighs, and my pumps squelched water. I tried mouth to mouth resuscitation, but it was no good. After checking the pulse, I knew that Eric Coventry was well and truly dead.

Bella licked my hand sympathetically, then careered away under the archway, barking. She obviously intended to fetch help, and before long, I saw a white and other-worldly figure appear. Its goldfish-bowl helmet was thrown back, and in no time at all I found myself enveloped by strong and comforting arms.

'Oh, Geoffrey,' I wailed, shuddering, partly from cold and partly from fear, and leaning gratefully against him. 'It's Eric Coventry, and he's dead!'

Chapter Ten

BARRY

When Dee didn't come back with Bella, I sauntered out to investigate, and soon found myself amongst a select little group by the pool – consisting of my bedraggled wife, Geoffrey Routledge, the hotel manager, Lissa, David Lydgate, who was offering moral support to Lissa, and two ambulance drivers who were carting away the body of Eric Coventry, on a stretcher still garbed as Julius Caesar.

Dee was having an argument with the hotel manager.

'It's no good saying he couldn't swim well, because he could – I've seen him. And there was bruising round the neck area. I noticed that as soon as I stopped trying to give artificial respiration. If you ask me, he was done in.'

The hotel manager was heard to mutter something to the effect that he wasn't asking her, and didn't want her far-fetched theories, thank you very much.

'Darling Dee,' Lissa put in pacifically, 'Eric had loads to drink earlier in the evening – you saw him in the dining-room, didn't you, David?'

'Oh yes, he had – enough to sink a battleship.'

'Only in this case it wasn't a battleship,' Dee pointed out tartly. There was an awkward silence.

'I admit,' Dee continued, in her 'I am being totally

rational, and I just want you all to know' voice, 'that it is conceivably possible Eric drowned while under the influence, having fallen into the pool and hit his head against the side. And I admit there was a cut on his head which seems to bear out this theory. All I'm saying is that I, personally, am not satisfied with this explanation, and I demand a full medical examination. Even an inquest.'

'By what authority, madam?' The hotel manager was gobbling like a demented turkey cock by this time. Dee smiled sweetly.

'Call it woman's intuition. Come, Bella. Barry.' And she sailed off, her sopping skirt held out in one hand, her head held high.

Bella, Geoff Routledge and myself in attendance.

'I require a drink,' Dee announced once back in our room. 'I have just been through a traumatic experience. So has Bella. I suggest hot whisky, in our room, after I've got out of this damned costume and had a hot shower. Geoff, you are welcome to join us. In fact, we might make it a sort of mini-conference. You won't see Ellen again tonight anyway,' she added. 'She went right off to bed after her performance.'

Duly installed, with Bella snug under a counterpane, but her head sticking out watching us, we began.

'Geoff, how did you come to be out there?'

Geoff blushed. After a lot of inarticulate gabbling, we gathered that some time after Ellen's performance he had taken himself off into the cool of the night to think romantic thoughts in a starry, rose-scented atmosphere, and had been wandering round for quite a while before Bella's yapping had alerted him and she had brought him to Dee's rescue.

'Exactly how long after Ellen finished, Geoff?'

He wasn't sure. He'd been talking to Linda Fairclough,

and he'd had a couple of last drinks with Ron. It could have been as long as half an hour.

'And you didn't see anyone else on your wanderings?'

Well, not really, that he could remember, though he'd think about it. You see, he'd gone off up the drive and some way along the roadway.

'And I take it you didn't have any motive to bump off Eric?' I laughed at Geoff's horrified expression.

'Don't worry, Geoff – we don't think you did it. But you must see that you were around and didn't have an alibi.'

'Dee, what makes you so sure Eric was killed by someone? It looked pretty much like an accident to me,' Geoff asked vaguely puzzled.

'That was what the murderer wants everyone to think, Geoff. We're going to have to wait for medical details, but my bet is Eric was killed before he ever hit the water.'

'Then it must have been someone strong,' I commented.

'Fairly strong, I imagine. But remember, Lissa and David both said that Eric had been drinking fairly heavily. In the dazed or euphoric state that would have produced, he'd be less able to put up a good fight, especially if the attack was unexpected, and came from behind him.' Dee crept up behind me and caught me in a stranglehold with her left arm. I struggled in vain, laughing, till she released me.

'You see?' She turned to Geoff.

'Yes, I suppose so. But *why*, Dee?'

Dee and I exchanged warning glances. We both thought Geoffrey was a sweetie, but he was too honest to be completely discreet. It would all come out, to Ellen or someone.

'Well that's just what we don't know exactly, Geoff. That's the job of the police to find out, once it's established he was actually murdered.' Geoff looked suspicious and unconvinced, and I can't say I blame him. After all, he knows I'm 'into this kind of thing' with my novels, and Dee was obviously into it up to her pretty neck, and suspecting more than she was telling. The atmosphere was a bit cool as he said goodnight, until Dee gave him a hug and said, 'You really are my hero, Geoff. I was feeling just terrible 'till you turned up and put your big strong arms round me.' He went off looking decidedly chuffed, and I said, 'I should have been there to put my big strong arms round you.'

'You can't be everywhere. But you can make up for it now.'

We got on the phone the next day, pestering the hospital and asking to speak to whoever had charge of the corpse of Eric Coventry. In due course, we found that the doctor was inclined to agree with Dee, taking into account the bruising she had noticed. And further seeking revealed that Coventry had had no water in his lungs when he died – which ruled out accidental drowning. Inspector Mitchell of the Gloucestershire Police Force descended on the Avondale, accompanied by his sergeant. We were the first to be called in. Inspector Mitchell was a somewhat morose Londoner who had married a Gloucestershire lass and transplanted. Several years later he was still missing 'the smoke'. It turned out he had known our old friend Det. Inspector Graves of the Yard, though tenuously, and had an admiration for him. Which was lucky, because it made him more tolerant of our interest in the case and our comments. We learned that pressure applied to the neck area to make Eric faint had in fact been overdone and he had passed out in every sense of the word – the murderer, obviously unaware of that, had bashed his head against the pool edge (where traces of hair and skin were

141

found) and dunked him in the drink. Where he no doubt would have drowned, if he had not been dead before hitting the water.

'So you see, Mrs Vaughan, you were right. Now, of course, we have to try to establish who and why. Perhaps you can help us there.'

Dee and I looked at each other. We were back in harness. Though we might not have been much further in establishing who or why, we did get some enlightenment as to when. According to Inspector Mitchell, time of death was provisionally set as somewhere between ten and midnight.

'That doesn't help us much,' Dee said to me. We were sitting on a grassy sward some distance away from the archery range – at least, I was sitting, Dee was reclining full length on her tummy. Bella was sniffing round in the undergrowth on the edge of the range.

'I mean – the Club members and guests were on the premises till eleven, so it could have been one of them.'

'You mean, another enemy of Eric's, who sneaked in to take a pot-shot at him?'

'More of a pot-push. Yes.'

'He should have been stabbed, really,' I complained. 'Caesar was stabbed.'

'Yes – by several people. Well, I shouldn't think it would be too difficult to round up a few would-be stabbers.'

'But we've only got one killer – unless you think one person applied the pressure to the relevant pressure points and the other shoved him into the water and bashed his head at the side of the pool. Good touch, that, by the way. If Eric had toppled in drunk, his arms and legs flailing any which way, he might well have conked his head against the stone edge round the pool.'

'I don't *think* it was two people. I think a meeting might

142

have been set up, by the pool, but the killer arrived early and concealed himself.'

'Where?' I was being difficult. Dee sighed.

'Use your imagination, Barry. Pressed flat against the hedge inside the archway. Or crouched down at the side of the club house. We could,' she offered, 'try it.'

'Later.' The pool was really a no-go area at the moment, and guests at the Avondale were still too stunned by the death, and further, the discovery that police were treating it as murder, to go anywhere near it. Which was leading to a lot of 'going-for-walks' and trips to Cheltenham, and renewed interest in riding and tennis facilities. And archery – the least popular of the sports and facilities on offer.

'What I really want to establish at the moment is "why?" and "who?" rather than "how?", which we basically know now anyway, thanks to Inspector Mitchell, the doctor and your persistence. As I see it, there are two leads.'

'Yes?' Dee leaned on her elbow, raising her top half and gazing at me earnestly. I cleared my throat and proceeded, in the voice I use to outline the finer points of international treaties, with my classes.

'One, the "outsider" theory. Which is pretty wide-open. It could have been a guest of a Club member, or a Club member, or, even worse, someone totally unconnected with the club and the hotel, who knew where Eric was staying, found out about the fancy-dress do, and set up a meeting and then bumped him off. Knowing Eric was such a loner, all he had to risk was someone coming into the pool area at the wrong moment, and if he kept a lookout, he could see that the coast was clear. If it wasn't, all he'd have to do was leave Eric's bumping-off to another day.'

'Yes. It figures. You mean one of his sleazy Soho contacts?' Dee asked.

'Or wherever. I imagine he had quite a few of them, dotted around. Maybe someone he'd double-crossed.'

'It could be *anybody*!' Dee wailed.

'Well, certainly only the police would be able to make those kind of enquiries. I imagine Inspector Mitchell has already seen the pitfalls and is cursing Coventry.'

'Who may be deriving some grim amusement from the situation, wherever he is.'

'Bad as he was, I suppose he's entitled to that,' I agreed. 'After all, he has been done out of his retirement.'

'The wages of sin,' Dee pointed out. 'You know, Barry, I agree with your "outsider" theory, and, unfortunately, if it's right, I think it's much more likely to have been a complete outsider rather than a Club member or guest. But if it was one of the latter . . . ' she paused. 'Well, there was the odd costume here and there which completely covered up the wearer. The White Rabbit, for example, if you noticed him. I mean, just think, if we didn't *know* it was Geoff inside that spaceman outfit, and he hadn't taken his helmet off from time to time, it could have been anyone.'

'I see what you mean. What about the one "guest" we do know had some connection with Eric?'

'You mean the weasel?' Dee smiled. 'Lissa found out that he's called Dougie Smith – of course that might not be his real name. But since he got in through Eric, who apparently asked the tennis lady to vouch for him as a special favour, he seems to have been an accomplice of Eric's, rather than an enemy.'

'Which isn't to say he likes Eric. He might have taken the opportunity to settle an old score. And Eric would trust him enough to meet him by the pool. Did you see him in the ballroom all, or most of the evening, Dee?'

'No,' she admitted. 'I just don't think it was him, that's all. Whoever did the dastardly deed must have been strong

144

physically, even if Eric was sozzled to the eyebrows. And have had a certain specialised knowledge to bring it off – even if it was bungled by overdoing things. Weasel just looked too weedy. What about lead number two, Barry?'

'I'm just coming on to that. But before we leave Dougie Smith, Dee, I suspect he may have been "doing" the bedrooms during the party. When I took the food to Bella, I heard someone close a door very quietly along the corridor. Which mightn't mean anything, of course, but when I came out again, another door was just slightly ajar, and as I walked down the corridor I got the feeling someone was watching me, waiting for me to go away. I didn't go back because at the time it didn't seem important – the first time could well have been someone going into their own room, and the second, a couple engaged in a bit of nookie, looking out to see if the coast was clear. But now . . . '

'Never mind, Barry. One's always wise after the event. The best thing is to try and find out if anything is missing. Really, it's Dougie Smith's bad luck we saw him in Malvern – otherwise we wouldn't have got suspicious when he turned up here, under Eric's wing. I did warn Lissa to keep an eye on handbags.'

'Well, lead two,' I continued. 'That concerns people in our party. There's more than one line of thought I've been following, but the most urgent one is the blackmail thing. Now, we know Stephen was being blackmailed by Eric, and we strongly suspect, from what I witnessd, that Karen was as well. I suspect they weren't the only ones. That gives both of them a motive. Did either of them leave the ballroom and dining-room during the relevant time, I wonder.' Dee frowned.

'Stephen did. So did Maddy. They were doing their Rhett and Scarlett thing for ages, then they both vanished.

And, come to think of it, Karen wasn't there either, for quite a while.'

'And they're both athletic enough and bright enough to have thought up the stunt with Eric and to have carried it out. Not necessarily premeditated, mind you. Both have hot tempers – something might have snapped. There's a sort of sense of *déjà vu* about that swimming pool. I can't help remembering the scene between Eric and Karen. Perhaps she agreed to meet him again there, to talk things over quietly and come to some agreement. And then lost her cool again, and flipped. As far as alibis for the others are concerned, well, we've only Geoff's word for it he was wandering around the road after Ellen's performance. And Ellen shot off after her performance. I agree Geoff seems incapable of guile, but you never know. If Eric had threatened Ellen, he just might have done it – he'd have had time. Suppose, for example, Eric had arranged to meet Ellen by the pool, and Geoff turned up instead.'

'I can't imagine what Eric might be blackmailing Ellen about,' Dee objected.

'Neither can I, but it could have been something completely untrue. I mean, he might have threatened to spread some scurrilous rumour. Ellen's reputation is pretty pure – a scandal would be disastrous to her image. Now how about the others. Was there anyone who wasn't there during the performance, or part of it?'

'Eric himself. I looked for his laurel-crowned head, and it wasn't in evidence. Nora Hilton was there all the time, and she went back to her booth after, for a spot more fortune-telling. So she's clear.' We caught each other's eye, and both started laughing at the thought of little sweet old Nora in a deadly armlock with Eric. When we'd recovered, Dee went on. 'Iris Forbes came in late – she cut the comedians and the trio, but got there for

Ellen. She glided in very quietly, like a grey ghost – if I hadn't been right at the back I wouldn't have noticed. She sat down quite near me. I think Andrew was there all the time, but he went off while we were dancing, afterwards. I think David Lydgate was there all the time, and Lissa was much in evidence, doing her thing, seeing everyone was happy. The Faircloughs went off together the same time we did after Ron's drink with Geoff, – I got the impression they were heading bedwards.

'Well,' I decided firmly, 'Inspector Mitchell will have to know about the blackmail attempts, but I don't want to do anything sneaky. 'I'll tackle Stephen and Karen, and give them the option of telling him themselves. Or rather, I'll tackle Stephen, you tackle Karen.'

Dee made an expressive grimace. 'Must I?'

I grinned. 'She is a pretty tough customer, isn't she? I don't think she'll dot you one, though. And I feel she'd talk more easily to a woman – especially if there's anything sexual Eric was holding over her.'

'OK,' Dee agreed reluctantly. 'You try and carry Stephen off at lunchtime, and I'll go for Karen.'

Lunch was a subdued affair to begin with. Then Andrew Forbes created a diversion by an argument with his wife. It appeared that a valuable diamond bracelet of hers had gone walkies. He was furious. She, however, did not seem unduly disturbed.

'Don't get so het up, darling – it's bad for your blood pressure. I'm positive no one's taken it. It had a weak clasp – it must have fallen off when I was wearing it yesterday!'

'But you weren't wearing it yesterday!'

'Yes, I was,' she put in quickly. 'I wore it to go and choose my costume – under a cardigan. And, come to think of it, I don't remember taking it off when

147

I got back. It must have slipped off in Cheltenham somewhere.' Andrew wasn't so philosophical about it. Well – an expensive diamond bracelet is an expensive diamond bracelet. Even if you are rich as Croesus.

'Is anyone else missing anything?' Lisa enquired anxiously. She murmured to us. 'Several people have phoned up the hotel complaining of money gone from handbags and pockets – I think you were right about Dougie Smith, Dee.'

Ron Fairclough said he couldn't find a wad of five pound notes he was sure he'd left in a drawer. Maddy Lang complained about a missing antique pendant, but admitted she might have mislaid it. The rest of us said we hadn't missed anything, but would look. By tacit consent, the subject of Eric Coventry's death was avoided, but there was a sense of strain, as if people were beginning to be aware that they were suspects, and some nasty and inconvenient questioning could be expected by everybody. The only one who made a direct reference was good old Ron Fairclough, who remarked, 'These goings-on are right up your street, Barry, aren't they? I mean, writing 'tec stories and that.'

'Hush, Ron,' Linda whispered, her face red, tugging at his sleeve. And there were general disapproving looks, as if someone had made a big gaffe – which of course, he had.

'Some people,' Maddy Lang was heard to state, 'don't know when to keep their big mouths shut.'

'Coming from her, that's rich,' Linda was scarlet with indignation.

'Don't take any notice, love,' Ron said comfortably. 'Sticks and stones, eh? Have some cake.'

The one safe subject was Ellen's performance, and under cover of the barrage of profuse congratulations, Dee drew Karen aside.

'Can I have a chat with you after lunch? I – um – want to ask you something.'

'Sure, anytime.' Karen obviously thought Dee was after advice about something. The publicity machine, perhaps. Or how to use one of the machines in the gym. I moved in on Stephen.

I caught Nora Hilton staring at me with bright, sharp eyes. She didn't miss much. Pity she had been in her booth most of the evening. Still, she might have a thought or two worth hearing. The Miss Marple of the 'Murder Weekend.' Dee and I might do worse than to have an exchange of opinions. At a later date.

'Stephen,' I began.

'I can guess. You want a word in my shell-like. And I can guess what about, too.' He sighed mournfully. 'Oh well – lead on Macduff. Bring on the tumbrils.'

'No tumbrils yet.' I slipped out the door, and he followed me, grabbing an apple *en route*.

Chapter Eleven

DEE

I drew Karen off to our room. There, I reasoned, she was less likely to walk off than outside. Besides, I could see Barry heading for the great outdoors with Stephen. I didn't want to cramp his style.

'So? How can I help you?' Karen took a seat by the window.

'Well . . . it's a bit awkward, Karen. We all want to get to the bottom of this Eric Coventry business, don't we?'

'Do we?' Karen shrugged, and tossed back her ash-blonde mane. 'Personally, darling, sorry to be callous and all that, but I found him a perfectly poisonous creature, and it would be hypocritical to pretend great concern over his death or who killed him. Sorry if I'm shocking you.'

'I'd a feeling you might say something like that. I thought he was a creep too, but even the creeps of this world have a right to their lives. To be blunt, Karen, you appear to be one of the people who had a motive for wishing him out of the way – a particular motive, I mean, not a general one.'

Karen raised an eyebrow, looked at me coolly, and drawled, 'Really, darling, and what might that be?'

Underneath the ultra-cool exterior I could sense a hint of tension.

'Blackmail? I should explain that Barry witnessed part of a scene near the swimming-pool where you slapped Eric's face and called him – now, what was it? "Crooked, conniving bastard", or words to that effect. You also stated you weren't going to do something he wanted you to. If not blackmail, how do you explain that, Karen?'

'Ah – the boy sleuth, skulking around.' I let that one pass. Karen was understandably a mite miffed. And we sleuths *do* skulk. From time to time. There is no point in denying it.

'Suppose I don't choose to explain it?'

It was my turn to shrug. 'You'd have to eventually – to the police. You see, if they don't examine leads, suspects can't be eliminated. Be practical, Karen. You've a business to run. You don't want to be held indefinitely, or remain liable to further questioning later on. If you didn't kill Eric, think of it as a bit of embarrassment in a good cause. If you don't want to tell me, fair enough. But I shall inform Inspector Mitchell of the incident – or march you in and leave you to tell him, if you'd prefer.'

'Oh, what the hell. Stop acting like a schoolmistress, Dee. I don't mind telling you, and I'll reveal all to the Inspector, if necessary. If it will help get me back to civilisation and away from this dump.'

Karen stood up and walked to the window – just a few paces, but she made the move dramatic. She stood with her back to me, looking out.

'I've had a client who wasn't satisfied with our services. Actually he isn't usually satisfied with anyone's. He's very hard to please. He took his business to another consultant. A year later, we lost another account. It wasn't a big one, and it didn't break us. We honestly had tried our best. Business is actually booming – it's a case of, you win some, you lose some. But Eric threatened to get one of those not-too-scrupulous press writers on to it – not directly, you understand, through someone who knows someone who knows the journalist. You know the kind of implication, Dee – that our firm is far less competent than it appears to be, and that all is not well. Not libellous, just pointing out facts that are true and dropping vague hints. Not even the kind of thing you can demand a written retraction for without drawing adverse comment. At the moment we're angling for another account – a really big fish. There are competitors. With Eric's threats our big fish would not sign up with us. At least, there's a strong danger of that. It could ruin my plans for further expansion. Of course, for a consideration – say five thousand, which I could afford – nothing more would be done. I was furious, of course, and threatened to go to the police, but Eric laughed and said he doubted I could prove anything, there being no witnesses, and he'd be out of the country soon anyway. That was when I shouted at him and hit him. End of scene.'

She took a deep breath and continued, 'However, not end of episode. I calmed down and approached him later – said I'd been thinking, and might be interested in a deal, but it would take time to get the funds. I was going to try and stall him. We agreed to meet by the swimming-pool again – at ten. It was a fair bet everybody would be watching the entertainment then. Well – I turned up, but he didn't. I waited for a bit, then sloped off. I went to his room, but he wasn't there. I was so fed up I didn't go back to the ballroom to check if he was still there. I reckoned he'd maybe got cold feet and decided to call the whole thing off. Eventually I settled down in my room with a book – and just dropped off to sleep. When I woke up it was the early hours, and I remembered we'd eventually agreed 10.15 to give stragglers a chance to get out of the way and into the show. Well, it was too late to do anything about it then. In the morning I learned he was dead. Naturally I was going to keep quiet about the whole thing, especially as I'd no alibi at all. No one saw me going to my room, as far as I know.'

She turned round and came towards me, with appeal in her eyes.

'I know it sounds a fishy story, Dee – but I needn't have told you about the pool, need I? I needn't have told you about any arrangement.'

'Well, Karen, you'd better tell Inspector Mitchell. Right now. At least it establishes one fact – that Eric was nowhere near the pool from ten to whenever you left – what, about 10.05?'

'More like 10.07, according to my watch. And by the time I was back at the house it'd be 10.10, or so.'

'And you didn't see anyone going towards the pool area? You're sure?'

She nodded.

'That means, if Eric kept the appointment, he must have slipped out from wherever he was just after you went in. Maybe he was a bit late. Everyone knew the Club members and their guests would be streaming out to their cars by eleven. Which means, Eric must have been killed some time between 10.15 and eleven. My guess is, either Eric had arranged another tryst at the pool, after he could have reasonably expected to have got rid of you, or, more likely, someone saw him sloping off on his lonesome and followed him. Or even, someone else went down to the pool, by chance, found Eric there, and took the chance to attack him. If he'd topped up with a drink from his minibar just before setting out, to give him Dutch courage, or whatever, on top of what he'd had earlier, he'd really be a sitting duck, in no condition to fight back.' Karen gave me a grudgingly admiring look.

153

'That's a very convincing scenario, Dee. I can just see it – like a film. Are you sure you didn't do it yourself?' I laughed.

'Not guilty. Now, what about braving Inspector Mitchell?'

'All right. It's a bit like a visit to the dentist, isn't it?'

I was allowed to stay quietly in the room while Karen said her piece. The Inspector was quite inquisitorial, and I felt sorry for self-possessed Karen, for once nearly reduced to tears. Afterwards I offered my theories about times, etc. and the Inspector nodded.

'Sounds feasible. We'll think about it, Mrs Vaughan. By the way, we've drawn in your Dougie Smith. A slippery customer, small fry but on the fringes of the big leagues. Coventry must have been crazy to let him in here to do his pilfering bit. But then, seeing that Coventry's dead, and in no position to do him, he's been singing. With what he's got on Coventry, it seems like the biter bit – there was one big robbery locally that Coventry was master-minding, and I reckon if we start digging into friend Coventry's past, we'd find a few more. Dougie hasn't been rash enough to put the finger on anyone else – but it's only a matter of time before the Yard come up with the answers, once an investigation is set in motion.'

'You mean Eric was a sort of criminal master-mind, and Dougie blackmailed him into introducing him here, for the pickings, as a sort of present before he pushed off for his retirement?' I was agog.

'And possibly let him in on some other job he wouldn't have been allowed to touch otherwise. He swears he's clean on the Cirencester one.'

'Eric must have been losing his marbles.' The Inspector grinned.

'Looks like it, doesn't it? Losing his touch, anyway.'

154

As I remarked later to Barry, the last-ditch black-mail attempts on Karen and Stephen seemed an out-of-character spurt of sudden greed for a man with the brain to master-mind jewel robberies. I was a bit surprised something very nasty hadn't happened to Dougie Smith. Or perhaps it would have done, if something nasty hadn't happened to Eric Coventry first.

'What happened about Stephen, Barry?'

'As soon as Karen issued from the little morning-room (which had been set up as a temporary office for the boys in blue) I shoved Stephen in. Accompanied by the fair Maddy, who represented his alibi.'

'You don't mean Stephen was willing to spill the gaff about his blue films and all in front of Maddy?'

'I do indeed. You're behind the times on the romance front, Dee.'

'So give.'

'Well, after Stephen and Maddy had been wowing everyone with their waltz for quite a while, Maddy felt rather faint, and decided to change into something more comfortable, so Stephen said he'd do the same. By this time, according to Stephen, their previous hostility has disappeared and they've discovered they're soul-mates in lots of ways.'

'The course of true love never did run smooth,' I interposed.

'It certainly won't run smooth if Stephen is seriously suspected of killing Eric Coventry. However, Maddy seems to alibi him for that. They slipped onto the terrace for a few moonlight kisses before they doffed their costumes, and then decided they'd had enough of the party and other people. So they went to their respective rooms, changed and then betook themselves off up the road for a few drinks at a pub called The HayWain, which was crammed with locals, and though

155

they managed to find a secluded table to themselves, they were in sight all the time. True, one might not be able to rely on Maddy as an alibi, as she's potty about him, but the landlord and various regulars can bear out the story – they both even indulged in a spot of darts-playing, so it could hardly have been more public. And apparently they were seen both coming and going from their rooms, so there's no way either of them could have been down at that pool.

'Everyone was thrown out of the pub at eleven, but they managed to stay on for a bit, talking to the landlord till he shut up shop, and on the way back Stephen unfolded his lurid past.'

'What was Maddy's reaction?'

'Not shocked, according to Stephen. She said she'd have done something similar if she'd had to, but was furious about Eric. Not enough to bump him off, though! And they got in the gates just as the ambulance was coming out – the driver had to swerve to avoid them, so again that can be verified.'

'I'm glad, Barry. I really like Stephen. I hope he's going to give all these vital details to the Inspector.'

'If he doesn't, Maddy certainly will. She had the light of battle gleaming in her eye!'

'I wonder if those two will make a go of it?' I mused.

'Who knows? It may fizzle out, as they go their separate ways to take up new engagements. On the other hand, Maddy's a determined girl, and really far better suited to Stephen the an Lissa, I think. He likes fireworks – Lissa's calm charm would get on his nerves after a while. Anyway, she seems to prefer David Lydgate, and I'm pretty sure he's in the market for a wife.'

'What a horrid expression! We women aren't cattle, you know.'

* * *

156

The late afternoon light wasn't too good, as we approached our old spot by the archery range. One of the archers was just drifting off, deciding to call it a day. The others stood poised for another crack at the target, and a hail of arrows flew through the air, just as a slim dark-haired figure shot across the range, pursued by Bella, who was yapping excitedly at this lovely new game.

'Watch out!'

She ducked as she ran across, and was clear of the target by the time the arrows reached it. But no – one arrow flew wide and struck her in the arm. With a yell, she fell to the ground, clutching her arm.

'It's Ellen!' Barry shouted as we rushed over. But the girl on the ground, though she was wearing an embroidered cheesecloth top identical to Ellen's, was Maddy Lang.

'Are you all right, Maddy?' I helped her to rise, and she smiled gamely.

'I'll live. Ouch – it hurts, though!' Norm was at her side.

'That was a damn stupid thing to do!' His handsome features were suffused with anger.

'I'm sorry, Norm, it was. Don't blame Bella,' she added, looking beseechingly at me. 'It's my fault – we were playing chasing games at the side there, and she got excited, and I just rushed off without thinking.'

Norm was examining the arm. 'Luckily these arrows are pretty blunt, for safety. There isn't even blood. But you'd better have it looked at.'

'I'll take her to the house.' This was Iris Forbes, looking pale and worried.

'Maddy, I think it was my shot that hit you. I'm most terribly sorry.' There was a protesting chorus from the other archers.

'How can you know it was yours, Iris? It could have been any of us.'

'I think it might have been mine, actually.' This from David Lydgate, looking equally pale and unhappy.

'Or mine.' A Club member, thickset and weather-beaten.

'Look, there's no point in speculating. It was an accident – right? Just get Maddy away and give her a cup of sweet tea,' I said. I looked at Karen Margolis, leaning, statuesque, on her bow. She neither claimed nor disclaimed the shot. I thought of her as Diana the Huntress, the night before, and my thought that she would wield a mean bow, and shivered. But why?

Iris led away an uncharacteristically subdued Maddy, nursing her arm, and I turned to Norm.

'Was that right, what you said? That it's not dangerous.'

'We-ell. It's not like a crossbow bolt.' We had read a murder case in the papers recently where one of those was used.

'It wouldn't kill her, certainly. Not unless coming at extreme velocity and hitting a vital spot. But, put it this way – she won't be able to play tennis again during her stay.'

Later we found a cheerful Maddy, her arm bandaged, being fed tea and toast by a strangely protective Stephen.

'Stephen seems to think I'm a piece of porcelain, anyway, Dee. Isn't it silly of him?' They exchanged a melting look.

'Stephen, much as I hate to interrupt love's young dream, how did the session with Inspector Mitchell go?'

'OK, I guess. He certainly seems to think I'm in the clear. And the first thing I'm going to do when I get back to London is make sure that *Sins of Don Juan*

158

print goes up in ashes – even if I have to raise a second mortgage to buy it!'

'Maddy,' I said, 'Norm was wrong. You *will* be able to play tennis again, if you want to. It's your left arm that's out of action.' Maddy shook her head.

'Norm was right. I'm left-handed, you see, Dee.'

Conversation proceeded along different channels, but I was left with a funny sort of niggling feeling at the back of my mind.

The incidents of the day were not yet over. An angry Geoff Routledge slammed into dinner, glaring at everyone. He seated himself at the table next to ours.

'What's up, Goeff?' Barry ventured at last. 'The Inspector been giving you a bad time?'

'I don't think that's funny.' The Inspector had been quizzing people right left and centre throughout the day. Causing depression all round. And somehow, this evening, we were all aware of the empty seat where Eric Coventry might have sat. Pity, and guilt, that we hadn't liked him. And the horrid knowledge that someone – perhaps one of us – had killed him. It was as if we expected him to suddenly appear, like Banquo's ghost, and point an accusing finger. The waitress glided in, with Geoff's soup, and he addressed himself to it. When he finished, he deigned to expand.

'It's Ellen.'

'What's the matter with her?'

'Everything. She was in floods of tears, poor little thing. Refused to come to dinner. She's having a tray in her room.' He glared at us as if we were directly responsible.

'What *happened*, Geoffrey?'

'She was playing badminton, over in the sports centre. Now that they've finished their investigations of the pool area, all the facilities are on tap again.' I nodded.

'She was playing with Stephen. He beat her hands down, and she decided to go on practising shots against the wall while he went off for his shower. Well, you know those badminton rooms.' I nodded again. They were large and somehow rather spooky, I'd thought, on the one occasion I'd gone round the area, looking in on them through the windows, from the balcony running around the top. Of course, they'd been deserted then.

'One thing you probably don't know about Ellen is that she suffers from claustrophobia. To be shut in anywhere, especially in the dark, gives her the screaming ab-dabs. Well . . . ' he paused, looking very grim, as the waitress brought his next course, then continued, 'Ellen was practising her shots perfectly happily, when suddenly she had the feeling someone was looking in on her from above. She couldn't see anyone, but she stopped, quite rigid, and she swears she could hear footsteps from up on the balcony, then a horrid low laugh. It went on and on, she couldn't tell if it was a man or a woman. Then the lights suddenly went out. All over the building. Someone had switched off the mains. Stephen found that later, when he got out of his shower and stumbled along to investigate. He switched them on again. But that was a while later – he had to grope his way around, and he could hear Ellen screaming and screaming in there.'

'God, how ghastly!' It certainly wasn't an experience I'd have relished.

'As you say, Dee.' I'd heard the expression 'mirthless smile' a lot of times. Now I was seeing one.

'Well, Ellen groped her way to the door. It was locked! And then she heard that terrible triumphant laugh again. She said it sounded demented – like the madwoman in *Jane Eyre* – only she still couldn't tell if it was a man

160

or a woman. She fainted, and the next thing she knew, the lights were on, and Stephen was bursting in. He got her over to her room, and calmed her down, then sent for me. She's tucked up in bed now, with her tray, and Maddy's keeping her company.'

'You mean, the door wasn't locked after all? Just wedged?' I questioned.

Geoff shook his head. 'I think whoever locked it unlocked it again, to make it seem as if it was just Ellen's fevered imagination. She says if it wasn't for the laugh, she'd think that too.'

I looked at Barry. He looked at me. We both looked at Nora Hilton, who was sharing our table. She had her 'fey' look.

'I'm afraid, dear Dee, there's a sense of evil in the air.'

We managed to soothe Geoffrey a bit, and after dinner I slipped off to see Ellen. She looked up expectantly as the door opened, and looked disappointed to see me.

'Sorry, I'm not Geoff, Ellen – but I don't think it's a respectable time to be visiting ladies' bedrooms.' That drew a wan smile.

'Barry and I sent him off to bed – otherwise he'd have been on sentinel duty. How are you feeling?'

'OK. Tired. Maddy's been an angel.' The 'angel' smiled.

'That's not what people usually call me!'

I chatted a bit, about naughty Bella, which amused them. Then I asked, gently, 'Just one thing, Ellen. What were you wearing this evening?' She looked puzzled.

'Just jeans – and a red shirt.'

'Thank you.' Ellen looked puzzled, but I didn't enlarge.

'I should think Maddy wants to go off to bed now. You're perfectly safe, Ellen. Lock your door if you want to. Remember, Barry and I are next door, and if you have a nightmare or anything, just come in to us.'

'Thanks, Dee. I'll be all right now.' She went on in a dreamy voice. 'Geoff really is wonderful, isn't he?'

'The best. I'd snap him up myself, if it wasn't for Barry! Come on, Maddy, bedtime.'

Out in the corridor, Maddy clutched my arm.

'Why did you ask Ellen that – about what she was wearing?' She looked frightened.

'I think you can guess. Lock your door, too, Maddy, won't you?' She nodded, and went off.

Back in our room, Barry said, 'It's not all to do with Eric Coventry, is it?'

'No. Too many incidents. The one with Iris may have been a blind – and I wouldn't be surprised if there's another, with another victim. Maybe Lissa, or me. Or even one of the men. Again, as a blind. But I think the real target is either Ellen or Maddy. The riding incident might have been aimed at either, or the incident this evening – apparently Ellen was wearing jeans and a red shirt, and we all know those are Maddy's trademark. Especially the colour red. On the other hand, it's Ellen who suffers from claustrophobia – but whoever did it may not have known that – so you see, it's fifty-fifty whether it was Ellen or Maddy. And as for the target shooting – well, it may have been a coincidental accident, but it seems a bit much to swallow. And Maddy was wearing a top identical to one of Ellen's – so again, which one?'

Bella grunted intelligently, and I scolded, 'Yes, you wicked little dog, and that was partly your fault!' She looked suitably chastened.

Barry was wearing burnt-orange silk pyjamas – a present from my sister Barbara.

'Those are hideous pyjamas, Barry.'

'Blame Barbara, not me.' I slid into bed beside him.

'You're nice and warm, though. Is Geoff safely bedded down for the night?'

'Yes – under protest.' We both laughed.

'He is a lovely man. I hope Ellen marries him and forgets the awful Jason and settles down to life on the farm.'

'Dee – I can see why Maddy, with her money, might be a target, and you may be right. If someone is acting against her, it might be on orders from someone. And that agent might have been blackmailed by Eric. But who – and why just frighten her? To drive her off her rocker or something? I really can't see why they have it in for Ellen.'

'I don't either, darling. By the way, Nora Hilton told me I was going to be near sudden death, when she told my fortune. And I found Eric. That's scary, isn't it?'

'It certainly is. Did she tell you anything else?' I smiled in the darkness.

'Nothing that won't keep. Goodnight, darling. Goodnight, Bella.' Bella snored gently.

Chapter Twelve

ANOTHER DEATH
DEE

We slept in pretty late the next day. Beside me, Barry stretched, yawned, opened a lazy eye, sat up, and fell back again.

'*Carpe diem*,' he remarked. Which, roughly translated, means 'enjoy it while you can'.

'I couldn't agree more. Breakfast in our room?'

'Breakfast in our room it is.'

I nipped along to see how Ellen was, but she'd already descended, leaving gusts of 'L'Air du Temps' behind, and a jumble of clothing on a chair at the foot of the bed. Hopefully, recovered from her ordeal. However, thinking back over the previous day's events made me thoughtful, and even more thoughtful when I thought back still further.

I was reviewing the scene in Iris Forbes' bedroom when something clicked on like a light in my mind. Barry was showering as I ordered breakfast from room service. I put the receiver down, slowly picked it up again, and got a long distance outside number.

'Anne? That you? It's Dee Vaughan. Listen, be a love and do something for me. Again. I know I'm

164

always asking you, but . . . ' At the end of the line a chuckle came.

'But that's what friends are for, right? OK, shoot.' Anne is a journalist ex-colleague. She gradually moved into big-league reporting after *Trends* folded up, and she is the world's best at ferreting out both considered and unconsidered trifles about anyone and anything.

'I want you to get me some background info. On David Lydgate. A young civil engineer, parents live in Jersey, works in Abu Dhabi. I gave the name of the firm.

'I want to know if he's ever had any connection with Langs, the big contractors. Oh, and Anne, another thing. Could you get me the low-down on one Iris Forbes, married to a Canadian haulage millionaire called Andrew Forbes. Chiefly her family background.'

'You don't want much, do you?' Anne complained. 'All right – I'm on holiday as it happens, but just mooching round. I suppose this is all to do with some sleuthing activity?' I confirmed it.

'Anything to help a hard-working gumshoe.'

Barry came out of the bathroom as I put the phone down, and room service tapped at the door. He looked suspiciously at my innocent face as I poured out coffee.

'Dee, you're up to something. Who were you phoning?'

'Just Anne.' I smiled angelically.

'I suppose that means you're sending the poor girl off on some wild-goose chase dredging the dirt on one or more of our fellow-guests.' I did not deny it.

'Apart from having access to press-cuttings files and henchmen to help her, Anne's got a network of contacts that would make the Mafia look like an old boys' club.'

'So who?'

'David Lydgate and Iris Forbes.' Barry nodded, and waited for me to expound.

'If some relation is out to injure Maddy, it's a possibility he's something to do with Langs. And it might tie in with her "expectations". David's a civil engineer, we don't know much about him except he's been working abroad. But he may have worked for Lang's sometime, or met someone from the family out in Abu Dhabi. He might have let them know Maddy was on this holiday, when she joined, and been given instructions. I know it's a bit thin, but, examine any angle.'

'And Iris Forbes?'

'Now, that lady intrigues me. I've been thinking back. Various odd things, like a sarcastic remark Eric made about her timing being good, after you and Lissa rescued her from the sauna.'

Barry caught on quickly. 'Yes – it was fortuitous she'd asked Lissa to come over and collect her. Lissa's the most conscientious of girls – if she hadn't been able to come herself, she'd have sent someone else over. My being there too was an unexpected bonus.'

'Making sure she'd be found in time. Eric sounded as if he thought the whole thing was a put-up job, though at the time I didn't think much about it. Now, if Iris was shielding herself, to make it look as if she was being victimised as well as Ellen and Maddy, then she may well have been responsible for Ellen's nasty time and Maddy's riding disaster – as for the archery incident, it was the easiest thing in the world to say she was responsible, and act horrified penitence. Of course, everyone would think it was an accident, and since no one was sure whose arrow it was, it was completely disarming. With Eric out of the way, she could continue with her campaign.'

Barry was looking sceptical. 'Dee, you'll have to do better than that. I agree with the sauna incident possibly being a put-up job – but that could have just have been some obscure form of attention-seeking. Aimed at making Andrew all protective and lovey-dovey, or something.

You're not seriously suggesting she killed Eric because he found out she was getting her kicks in sadistic little games frightening the younger, more attractive women?'

'I don't think it's as simple as that, and several people could have killed Eric. But she's a strong, athletic woman, with medical knowledge, and she was out of sight during some of the relevant time. Moreover, in that greyish get-up, particularly with the cloak round her, she could have slipped away into the dark like a shadow. I think Eric was blackmailing her. Remember that packet we saw him posting? And remember Iris's missing diamond bracelet, and her very, pat explanation. It's my vet that bracelet never turns up in Cheltenham or at the hotel.'

'But why? Why blackmail her? It just doesn't make sense, Dee.'

I poured out myself more coffee, and drained it.

'It's beginning to, to me, though I'm still pretty muddled in my mind. Iris was at the riding school for the morning session. She knew the layout, the routine and the horses. She could have slipped out and set up the wool trap, and slipped the burr under Snuggles' saddle later. If Eric was out walking by the riding school, he could have seen her setting up the trap, and taxed her with it later, after Maddy's accident. He wouldn't even have to have known or guessed *why* she did it – if it came out, it would irretrievably tarnish her image, including in Andrew's eyes. She might have agreed to pay Eric's price, but not trusted him not to come back for more. After all, she's rich pickings. It doesn't mean she killed him, but it gives her a motive, and at the least, it supplies another blackmail victim.'

'What motive could Iris have for harming Maddy? Hardly in cahoots with some ghastly relative of Maddy's, for cash.'

'True, oh sage one. But you see, I don't think she

intended to frighten and possibly injure Maddy. I think it was Ellen – who would have had Snuggles as a mount, until we found Maddy was a nervous rider, too.'

'That's even harder to believe. And, Dee, Ellen's an artist – a highly imaginative, highly-strung girl. We know from Geoffrey she's terrified of being shut in anywhere. Couldn't the mains in the sports centre have been switched off by mistake – say by the odd-job man – and Ellen *imagined* the spooky laugh – you know how scary it is being in the dark. And even Stephen admits the door was *unlocked* when he got there.'

'That's what Iris intends everyone to think. And remember, it's only us who suspect the archery incident might not be an accident. Which leaves the riding incident – again, neatly explained by the idea of malicious schoolchildren. It's all beautifully vague – and no one has been killed or even badly hurt; the worst is bruises and a stiff arm for Maddy. As you say, it's all too thin, unless it's part of a campaign to harass, bewilder and generally torment Ellen Starr. Since Ellen is so essentially harmless, I see the motive there as being one of active malice and possibly revenge, carried out by someone practical, quick-thinking and able to plan well. Which fits Iris.'

'Now listen, Barry. At lunch, a while back, Ellen was rabbiting on to Geoff about her mother, Jeannette Stark, a concert pianist. Iris spilt her wine all over the table. She passed it off very quickly and gracefully, and of course I didn't think anything of it, but later I got to thinking that the name Jeannette Stark meant something to her, and she knocked over her wine in shock. Ellen's mother would be about the same vintage as Iris – she's dead now, but if she were alive she would. Another thing – another piece of the puzzle that came to me a few minutes ago – is a photo I saw in Iris's room. It was of a young version of Iris, dressed in tennis gear, and I

168

made some remark about how pretty Iris had been when she was younger. She made a peculiar sound, and looked peculiar altogether – at the time I thought it was because she thought I was making odious comparisons between her younger, beautiful self and her older self. But then, with the discovery that Maddy is left-handed, it came back to me that the girl in the photo was holding her racquet aloft in her *left* hand. Iris is right-handed. Also, it's an odd thing to have a photo of oneself on show with family photos, unless it's a recent one or part of a family or school or college group.'

'You mean,' Barry said slowly, 'it could have been the photo of a cousin, or sister?'

'Twin sister, probably, she was so like Iris in features. And we know how close twins are reputed to be. Suppose – just suppose, Barry – and I know it's a long shot – that this Jeanette Stark had done something nasty to Iris's sister, either wittingly or unwittingly, in the dim and distant. The mother is safely dead, but all of a sudden, she comes upon the daughter, beautiful, talented, famous, well-off, admired, and with an exceptionally nice young man in tow. It would only be human to feel dislike and resentment – and from that, it's just a few steps to trying to make Ellen pay in some way for whatever her mother did.'

Barry was now looking worried.

'Crazy though it sounds, I think you might be onto something, Dee. I suppose you should tell Inspector Mitchell.'

'Not without something more solid. You said yourself it sounds crazy. I'll see if Anne can come up with any info. And of course, there's the David Lydgate line to explore too.' Barry shook his head dismissively.

'I think Maddy is a red herring. While we wait, I'm going to pump Andrew about the photo. I might be able to get something on Iris's background from him as well.'

'Good idea. But make it very casual – the last thing I want is for Iris to think I suspect her.'

As it happened, we were having coffee mid-morning, in the coffee lounge, when Iris and Andrew strolled in, and they joined us. The conversation ran upon their interviews with Inspector Mitchell. Andrew was restive.

'The holiday's nearly up, and we'd planned to visit friends in Devon, before setting off on a cruise. I only hope we can get away soon.' Barry pointed out that police investigations took no account of personal inconvenience.

'I hope it's cleared up too, pretty quickly. I've a month's solid writing to do on a new book, before my new term starts, and Dee's due back at the office.' This led to more chat on the subject of Barry's books, and our respective jobs, and Andrew's property interests.

'Anyway, I don't suppose either of you two are seriously under suspicion.'

'Well, we had a bit of trouble accounting for our whereabouts, but I don't think the Inspector seriously thinks we had any motive. It was probably one of the man's criminal associates. He seems to have been a particularly ugly customer. Certainly *not* the kind of person one expects to find in a setting like this.' We agreed, and I turned the conversation to the various romances flourishing between the young people in our party. Iris smilingly agreed that they all seemed well-suited, and how nice it was to see romance was not dead. Barry commented on Ellen's performance, and again, there was not change in atmosphere.

'Of course,' I said, 'that kind of gift is often inherited, in some form or other. I believe her mother was a well-known concert pianist in her youth. Jeanette Stark. I can't say I've ever heard of her. Have you?'

170

I observed Iris closely, and there seemed to be the faintest flicker round her mouth, then she shook her head smilingly.

'I'm afraid I'm not well up on the musical scene.'

'How can you say that, Iris!' Andrew exclaimed. 'Why, while we were courting, she used to drag me to just about every concert and ballet there was, as well as plays, plays and yet more plays!' He rolled his eyes to heaven humorously. 'Will I ever forget that Shaw season! I like *Pygmalion* but the rest were a pain in the ass, frankly.'

'Philistine!' Iris was laughing. 'Oh, I know I love music, but I always forget the names of performers. Anyway, when I was young I was too busy establishing myself in my career. I just didn't have time for such luxuries.' She stood up. End of conversation.

'I'm going for a workout in the gym. I promised Karen I'd be there. Coming, Andrew?'

'Not yet, dear. I've got some letters to write.'

'Dee?'

'I'll take a rain-check, Iris. Actually, I'm waiting for a phone call.' Which was true enough.

I left Barry with Andrew, and wandered up to my room. I didn't expect Anne would get back to me so soon, but I kept myself occupied writing out a list of events and times, as far as I remembered them, since we'd been at Avondale. Good discipline. I went to lunch late, and found just Nora Hilton there. We chatted vaguely, avoiding the subject of Eric Coventry, but again dwelling on the romances that had sprung up.

'You know, dear,' she said, out of the blue, 'I don't think Mrs Forbes likes Ellen.'

'Why ever not, Nora?'

'I don't know, dear. It's just the way I've seen her looking at her sometimes.'

'Well, she doesn't like fortune-tellling, anyway. She positively refused to go and consult you. Said she didn't hold with that sort of thing.'

'Probably afraid of what I'd see,' Nora remarked. 'Not,' she added hastily, 'that I'm saying Iris has done anything dreadful. But everyone has secrets – some of them quite harmless, but one wants them to stay secret. Don't you agree?'

I agreed.

Barry returned mid-afternoon, exhausted, after a work-out with Norm and Andrew.

'I found out about the sister,' he told me. 'You were right – she was a twin. Her name was Eleanor, and she and Iris were very close, especially after their parents were killed in a car crash. Iris was the strong one, and the strong-minded one. Eleanor was always delicate, and Iris fussed over her like a mother hen. Incidentally, Eleanor was a musician – violinist, and a promising one. But she was subject to fits of depression, and after some unfortunate affair, she died tragically. Carbon monoxide fumes in a garage.'

'Suicide?'

'A verdict of accidental death was returned. Iris never speaks about it now, but she likes to remember Eleanor as the young, pretty, happy girl she used to be. A tragic story, really. Andrew doesn't know any of the details – who the man was, or anything.'

'I'm surprised he talked so freely to you about it.'

'I don't think he would have done, but he's worried about Iris. You see, she always gets moody round the time of Eleanor's birthday – which is today. Another reason Andrew wants to get her away from here and distract her from morbid concerns. I offered my sympathies, of course.'

'It's not going to be any picnic for him if my suspicions are right.'

'Where's Ellen, by the way?'

'Out on a picnic, with Geoff, Stephen and Maddy. She told Nora Hilton she wanted to try the jacuzzi later – which is something I'd like to do, too. I'm still waiting for Anne's call.

Which came in the early evening.

'Nothing on David Lydgate, Dee. No connection with Langs at all. Clean as a whistle.'

'What about Iris Forbes?'

'Clean as a whistle, too, dear. Quite hoi-polloi now, of course, but used to be a well-respected and hardworking nurse here before she emigrated to Canada and continued her career there, marrying Andrew Forbes, a private patient, and retiring from the wards.'

I knew all this before. 'Family Background?'

'Rather tragic. Parents died in a car smash, leaving very little money and Iris and her sister had to fend for themselves. The sister was a music student, and became a violinist with the LSO. She had an ill-starred romance with a young man called René Saunders. Half-French, also a violinist, but a very gifted one – became a soloist. He ditched her for a girl called Jeannette Stark, a promising concert pianist. The whole thing was tragic. Eleanor died – there were rumours of suicide, but a verdict of accidental death was passed. René later died himself – of leukaemia. The Stark girl came out of it all right – she married a year later, to one James Hawkins, a very ordinary sort of chap, had a little girl and faded out of the musical scene into dull domesticity, eventually. Hardly surprising Iris chose to emigrate, with all those sad memories here. Well – anything else you want?'

'Not just now, Anne. Thank you. You've been a great help.'

'Always glad to be of assistance. Let's meet up soon and chew the fat.'

I agreed to do that.

'Well?' Barry demanded impatiently. I told him.

'We ought to tell the Inspector.'

'I think he's "in conference" with someone or other. Something to do with Eric. I'll leave you to pass on the info., Barry. I'm going to hunt up Ellen, and stay glued to her side.'

'You'll have a job. She's out jogging with Maddy – the others came back,but those two headed off somewhere.'

'Well, I'll go and look for them.'

By the time I'd located Maddy, wandering along a side lane, it was dusk.

'Where's Ellen?'

'She got tired and headed back. She said she was going to try the delights of the jacuzzi. Hey, Dee, where are you off to? *Dee!*'

The balcony overlooking the jacuzzi was laid out with white chairs and tables. Linda Fairclough, wearing a swimsuit, was sprawled out on one chair, her feet on another, nursing an orange squash. She greeted me.

'The jacuzzi's great, Dee – but you haven't got your swimsuit!'

'I forgot it. Have you seen Ellen?'

'Sure I have. She was splashing round for ages with Iris Forbes. They were laughing like mad – drinking, too.' She indicated two glasses and a large bottle by the side of the jacuzzi pool.

'It was full, and now it's empty. Iris didn't have much

174

– Ellen polished off the whole bottle, nearly!' Linda sounded disapproving.

I slipped down to the lower level. There was some liquid left in one of the glasses. It was amber coloured, and gave off a distinctive fragrance – almonds, fruit spices.

'1001 Nights,' I breathed. If Ellen had polished off nearly a bottle of that heady concoction, she must be well and truly paralytic by now.

'Where did they go, Linda?' She stared, puzzled by the urgency in my voice.

'Back to the house. Oh – Ellen was saying something about wanting to see the view from the parapets, and would Iris go with her, and Iris said, no, she didn't want to, but if Ellen insisted she'd show her the way, because it's down a little corridor that's hard to find. She did say she thought Ellen ought to go and lie down instead, though.'

'I'll bet she did!' I muttered savagely. Iris Forbes was good at covering her tracks.

'Linda – I'm going up there. Will you please, *please* rush over to the house and try and round up the Inspector. And Geoff, if you see him, and any of the other men. Not Andrew, though. Tell them Ellen's up on the parapets roaring drunk and it's dangerous, and they must get her away. It's vital. Linda?'

'Like this?' Linda indicated her swimsuit uncertainly.

'Yes, *yes*, Put your robe and slip-ons on. And HURRY!'

'Oh, all right.'

I shot off, not waiting for her. Time was of the essence. I only hoped I wouldn't be too late. Poor, naive Ellen – how she had played into Iris's hands.

The stairway to the parapets was dark, tortuous, narrow, and I had to put a hand against the wall to support myself. Up and up it went, round and round. I was feeling dizzy, and my heart was thumping. At last I got to the final steps and pushed open the wooden door that led out onto the little pathway. Beyond the crenellations, in the dusky light, I could see the view to the racecourse. The path wound round, widening to a little square. Down below, there was a courtyard, in the open centre part of the building. The rooms were dark down there, except for one, where a light glowed.

Then I saw them. Two figures, grappling, against the stone barricade. It was low, and crenellated too. For a moment I stood immobile. The taller of the two – they were both in white towelling robes – had a firm grasp of the other, and seemed to be pushing her backwards, bending over. There were harsh gasps and grunts. It was a death struggle in every sense of the word. And what chance did Ellen, physically weaker, and muzzy-headed, have against Iris?

I moved towards them, afraid to call out or make a sound. If I could just get in there and grab Ellen away . . . but any move might precipitate Iris into a final, desperate push. A stone broke loose and fell, shattering with a horrid sound down below on the cobblestones. And there was another sound – pounding feet, and yells. As Geoff burst through the wooden door, followed by the Inspector, Barry and David Lydgate, Iris paused, and seemed to relax her hold.

With a superhuman effort, Ellen shoved her away and broke from her grasp. She ran, staggering, towards me, as Iris teetered, and, with the impetus of Ellen's shove, toppled, clawed at the air to right herself, and then, slowly, disappeared through a gap in the stone. There was a terrible scream, and a dull thump, and then nothing could be heard but Ellen's terrified screams. I caught her in my arms, and murmured soothing things, then I was pushed away, and Geoff took over.

'It's all right, darling. You're all right. Don't look. Just come with me.' He picked her up in his arms, and carried her down the winding staircase. The rest of us stood huddled together, staring down at the prone form spreadeagled on the stones below.

'Send for an ambulance. At once.' Inspector Mitchell spoke curtly to David, who nodded and set off down the stairway. 'But I'm afraid it's too late.'

Chapter Thirteen

FINALE
BARRY

It was indeed too late. Iris Forbes was dead on impact, her skull cracked. Her body was taken away. Later, the devastated Andrew Forbes would have to arrange a funeral. And later, he would have to hear everything.

Inspector Mitchell was angry with Dee and myself, for not speaking out sooner. If we had, and it was a sobering thought, that terrible scene might not have taken place. But, as Dee pointed out to me, it was surely better that Iris should die than stand trial for the murder of Eric Coventy.

Once she had recovered from sedation, Ellen proved most informative. Iris, she said, seemed to have gone mad suddenly. One moment she was talking naturally to Ellen, and remarking on the view, the next she had pinioned her against the wall and held her there in a vice-like grip, while she told her what her mother had done to Eleanor.

"'And it's her birthday today, Ellen,' she had said in conversational tones. 'So you see, I have to kill you. An eye for an eye – a daughter for a sister. At first I just meant to frighten you – and maybe hurt you a little.

Put you out of action for the holiday.' And it had all come out – the riding accident, how she had rigged up the trap, and planted the burr under the horse's saddle, and how Eric Coventry had blackmailed her.

'"And you see, Ellen, I knew I might have to kill you later, so I couldn't risk him being around. I guessed by that time he was a criminal and I thought with luck it might be decided one of his enemies might have got into the hotel and killed him. Anyway, I had to risk it.' And then the archery incident – 'I thought it was you, Ellen, not Maddy, and I hated you so much I couldn't resist letting fly. Not you personally, Ellen, but your mother's daughter. I don't want you to think it's personal. Anyway, you've had a good enjoyable life – more than my poor Eleanor had."

'And then she described how she locked me in that badminton room – and she laughed, like she had then. I knew she was mad, then, and I had to get away, so I started struggling, but she was too strong for me. I didn't even scream – I had to save all my strength for struggling. She said, "It'll look like an accident – Linda knows you had a lot to drink, and it'll look as if you turned dizzy and fell. The wall is loose here, I'll loosen it some more. Linda heard me say I wasn't coming up with you, and I'll act *so* distressed, and blame myself for not accompanying you. Everyone will believe me, wait and see."'

Ellen shuddered and looked wild-eyed for a moment.

'It's all a bad dream, darling,' Geoff said, 'and when you wake up I'll be there to take care of you for ever. You're coming back with me for a nice rest after all this, and you'll soon forget it ever happened.' Dee and I exchanged a smile.

'In the midst of darkness, there is light,' she whispered to me. 'Shall we leave them to it?' We did.

*   *   *

The time came for us all to pack up our baggage and leave. Andrew Forbes had already gone, to another hotel. Poor man – the papers would have a field day. 'Millionnaire's Wife Murders Crook! Death Struggle with Famous Pop-Star at Dusk!' One could just imagine the lurid headlines. Fortunately Canada was far away enough for it not to hurt his business or his sons too much.

'Still, I feel very sorry for him,' I said. 'He adored Iris – and funnily, apart from her thing about Ellen and Jeannette, she was an eminently sane and practical person.'

'Well, Eleanor was the strongest emotional tie she had in her life, even including Andrew. And, after money and the *crime passionel*, revenge is one of the strongest of motives.'

'You sound like Stephen and Maddy, pulling Shakespeare to bits,' I complained. Dee laughed.

'What are they going to do?'

'Go back to London. Stephen starts work on his *Baron* series soon, and Maddy has to see her agent. I gather she hopes for some good parts in rep.'

'Goodbye, Lissa,' Dee said, as we stood in the hallway prior to departure. 'Thank you for looking after us so well – sorry it's been so traumatic for you.'

'Well, actually, Dee, Barry, I've had enough. I hardly like to announce an engagement after – well, recent events, but the fact is, I'm going to meet David's parents and subject to their approval, we're hoping to have a quiet wedding at the end of the summer, then I'll go back to Abu Dhabi with him.'

'Congratulations! We're so glad for you both.' Dee kissed her.

'Excelsior Holidays will just have to get along without

me, I'm afraid. I expect I'll find something useful to do in Abu Dhabi, though.'

We bade an especially fond farewell to Nora Hilton.

'And don't forget my prediction,' she said to Dee, a beguiling twinkle in her eye.

'You know, I think she'd have worked out the answers eventually,' I remarked. 'But we got there first.'

'Yes – she's good at solving fictional crimes – but we're better at the real thing.'

'What did she mean about her prediction, by the way?'

'Oh – nothing much.' I sighed. When she likes, Dee can out-do the Sphinx any day.

'I don't see how Ellen can possible turn Geoff down now.'

'Me neither. You know, in a way she'll be following in her mother's footsteps. I mean, giving up her musical career and marrying a nice, but ordinary man.'

'Well, there's always her songwriting.'

'Yes, there is that.'

We put the luggage in the boot, climbed into Hotspur, and I started the engine.

'One murder, one near-murder, one accidental death, blackmail and various odd incidents,' I remarked. 'I really can't wait to get back to the peace of Woodfield.'

'Where Zoe will be waiting to tell us all about her sunny times in Turkey.' I groaned.

'But even that would be comparatively restful.'

Bella stuck her head out of the window. She isn't sure quite what's been going on, but she knows she's been neglected the last couple of days. She surveyed the impressive frontage of Avondale Country Club, as we set off. The scent of roses was in the air, and a couple of Club members were playing tennis on the courts. Shouts and laughter came from the swimming pool. Bella looked at this peaceful scene with disdain.

'Woof-umph-harrumph-*Woof*' she declared. Which, roughly translated, means, 'I'm glad to get the hell out of this place.'

As usual, Bella had the last word.